HIGH PRAISE FOR
ROBERT J. RANDISI

"Randisi always turns out a traditional Western with plenty of gunplay and interesting characters"

—Roundup

"Each of Randisi's novels is better than its entertaining predecessor."

—Booklist

"Everybody seems to be looking for the next Louis L'Amour. To me, they need look no further than Randisi."

—Jake Foster, Author of *Three Rode South*

"Randisi knows his stuff and brings it to life."

—Preview Magazine

"Randisi has a definite ability to construct a believable plot around his characters."

—Booklist

BLOOD TRAIL TO KANSAS

ROBERT J. RANDISI

LEISURE BOOKS NEW YORK CITY

A LEISURE BOOK®

June 2007

Published by special arrangement with Golden West Literary Agency.

Dorchester Publishing Co., Inc.
200 Madison Avenue
New York, NY 10016

ISBN-10: 0-8439-5799-9
ISBN-13: 978-0-8439-5799-0

Printed in the United States of America.

Visit us on the web at www.dorchesterpub.com.

BLOOD TRAIL
TO KANSAS

CHAPTER ONE

Culverton, Montana

Dan Parmalee's reputation as a "cold" man was not something he deliberately cultivated. Rather, those who observed his normal demeanor—calm, expressionless, emotionless—deemed him to be "cold." Hence, the name. And while he did not cultivate it, he certainly did nothing to dissuade it. If people chose to believe that he was cold, and because of that chose to leave him alone, he was very satisfied with that.

For one thing, it served him very well when he was playing poker.

Parmalee had been in Culverton exactly ten hours, and he had spent a good portion of that time right here in the Four Bits Saloon. He had been there long enough to hear the story of how the owner, Nick Abel, had gone into a poker game with exactly four bits to his name, and had ended up winning the saloon, which he then renamed the Four Bits.

Parmalee was in no danger of winning it away from Abel. He was not playing in one of the house games, but rather in a pickup game that had been in progress when he had entered the saloon six hours ago, at two P.M.

At that time the saloon had been more empty than filled, but now, at eight P.M., the place was packed. Not only was the pickup poker game in progress, but two house games had been set up, as well as a faro table and a blackjack table. Culverton had not been overly impressive to Parmalee when he had ridden in at ten A.M., but the Four Bits had certainly impressed him. It appeared well managed and was well stocked with pretty girls—and shotgun guards on raised platforms. The bar was so long it took two bartenders to handle it. If Culverton ever grew into its saloon, it would be a hell of a town.

After six hours of playing, the gamblers had changed—only two of the original five players remained—and the stakes had doubled. Even so, it was still only a dollar and two game, but Parmalee had been able to build himself a couple of hundred dollars of profit. Poker, he believed, was a game in which you had to grind out your profit. Usually, he played for ten hours or more, and he never bothered butting heads with another player on a "big" pot. Very often the winner of a big pot let down his guard and went on to lose a few hands after that. Parmalee watched for players like that, and he had found one in this game.

The man's name was Gates, and when he took

in a sizeable pot, he whooped and hollered and let everyone know about it. Two or three hands later he was still thinking about it, and Parmalee usually took those hands.

When Parmalee had first sat in on the game, he had filled the table out to four men. Of the original three, only Charlie Battles remained. Charlie, he had learned by listening, was a sort of unofficial deputy in town. The town sheriff had two deputies, but when he needed a third, he usually called on Charlie. In the meantime, Charlie gambled. He was a good, steady player, and he had built himself a small stake, as well.

The other players—Gates, Alby Pearson and Dave Myers—had all joined the game later, at different times. Myers was a storekeeper, and Pearson and Gates were ranch hands from a nearby spread.

As ten P.M. rolled by, Gates started to get a confused look on his face. He knew that he had taken most of the big hands in the game since he had sat down, and yet he wasn't winning. On the other hand, Parmalee had not even taken part in those hands, and he was winning.

That just didn't sit right with Gates.

"I'm gonna get a drink," Gates said as the deal passed to Charlie Battles. "Alby, come get a drink with me."

"But I ain't—"

"Come on!"

Pearson nodded to the other players and stood up, saying, "Uh, I think I'll get a drink."

Gates and Pearson walked to the bar, where they stood and talked to two other men.

"You watchin' this?" Battles said to Parmalee.

"Uh-huh."

"Gates is starting to get real confused."

"I noticed."

"Just so's you noticed," Battles said, and didn't say another word. Dave Myers had listened to the exchange between Battles and Parmalee, and now *he* was confused.

Joey Shea knew she was going to get in trouble for this. Whenever she sneaked out of the house after dark and came to town, she got into trouble; but usually something exciting happened while she was in town, and that made the punishment worth it.

At that moment, ten-year-old Joey was crouched down outside the saloon, peering beneath the batwing doors. This, she knew, was where the excitement usually took place.

Parmalee watched as Gates and Pearson exchanged words with two other hands, both of whom looked over at the table at Parmalee. They were certainly making no secret of what they were talking about—at least, not to anyone with at least one working eye. To make it even more ludicrous, Gates and Pearson came back without drinks.

"Can we get on with the game now?" Myers asked.

Gates looked at Battles and said, "Deal."

Battles dealt, and as luck would have it, Gates, Myers and Battles ended up raising and reraising, while Parmalee sat the hand out. In the end, Gates came out with the winning hand. He whooped and hollered and raked in his chips, and proceeded to lose the next six hands—three of them to Parmalee, two to Battles, and one to Myers. At that point he realized that the money he'd won in the big hand was almost gone.

"All right, hold it!" He slapped his big hand down on the table, covering most of the cards so that they couldn't be gathered up.

"Excuse me," Parmalee said, "but it's my deal."

"Ain't nobody dealin' nothin' until we get somethin' straightened out."

"Like what?" Battles asked.

"Like why I ain't winnin' any money here."

Battles smiled and said, "Maybe it's because you're such a bad player."

Although it was Battles who was speaking, Gates seemed most put out by Parmalee, and the fact that Parmalee wasn't even talking to him seemed to make it worse.

"Whatayou got to say, friend?" Gates asked Parmalee.

Parmalee stared at Gates for a long moment—long enough for Alby Pearson to get a chill from the look in his eyes—and then said, "If you can't stand losing, you shouldn't play."

"I can stand losing, all right—"

"That's good," Parmalee said, interrupting him, "because the way you play, you must do a lot of it."

Gates glared at Parmalee. The aggravated gambler was a big, barrel-chested man who drank too much beer, and it showed in his belly. Still, he had bulging biceps and was no doubt a very powerful man. He also had three other men there to back him up.

Dan Parmalee was a tall, rangy man with large hands and long legs. He had dark hair that curled up around his collar, and he wore a neatly trimmed mustache. His eyes were slate gray, surrounded by crinkly lines at the corners. He had spent most of his forty-one years outdoors, and it showed in the lines and color of his face.

Charlie Battles, seated next to Parmalee, was half his size, but Parmalee could see that there was no back-down in Battles.

"Ease up, Gates," Battles said. "Just 'cause you're losin' and frustrated about it, don't let that push you into—"

"Shut up, Battles," Gates said. "I ain't talkin' to you."

"Hey," Battles said, putting both his hands up in front of his chest, palms out, "I'm just tryin' to keep you alive."

"I don't need no help with that," Gates said. He seemed to have forgotten that he had three men backing his play.

Battles leaned back in his chair and watched Gates.

"What's your beef, Gates?" Parmalee asked.

"I'll tell you what my beef is, friend," he said. "I'm the one winnin' the big hands here, nobody else, and still I ain't ahead. You don't even play the big hands, and you're winnin'. Why do you suppose that is?"

"You just explained it, Gates."

"Huh?"

"I don't play the big hands," Parmalee said.

"I'm not throwing money into those hands, so I'm not losing. I do, however, play the other hands, and I win a lot of them."

"A lot of little hands."

"Right."

"But I win the big hands."

"Right again."

"Whataya mean, right?" Gates asked. He was getting even more confused. "You just said I'm winnin' all the big hands. So how come I ain't winnin' and you are?"

Parmalee looked at Battles, who just shrugged.

"Gates," Parmalee said, slowing, "I win more hands than you do. It's the man who wins the most hands what wins most of the money."

Gates frowned, then shook his head. "That ain't right."

"Sure it is," Parmalee said.

Gates looked at Pearson and said, "That sound right to you?"

"Uh—" Pearson stammered.

Gates frowned, then looked at Parmalee and said, "You're cheatin'."

A hush fell over the table, and over the two nearby tables who overheard the word "cheatin'." Suddenly, everyone in the place seemed aware that something was happening at a certain poker table.

At the bar, the bartender leaned over to one of the girls and said, "Get Nick."

She nodded and hurried off.

The bartender motioned to a man standing at the bar and said, "Get the sheriff."

"Sure thing."

At the table, Parmalee's gray eyes looked even colder than usual.

"What?" he said.

"You heard me," Gates said. "The only way you could be winnin' more hands than me is if you're cheatin'."

"Gates," Battles warned, "you're askin' for a bullet."

"I don't kill that easily," Parmalee said to Battles. "Gates, put your gun on the table."

"What?"

"Do it."

"Whataya—"

"I'm going to put mine on the table," Parmalee explained, "and then we'll settle the question of cheating without guns."

"What?"

"There's no reason for anyone to get killed here," Parmalee said. "It's just a dispute over a card game."

Gates' eyes narrowed, and he leaped to a conclusion that was totally wrong.

"You're yella!"

Battles closed his eyes and said, "Oooh," to himself. He pushed his chair back from the table, ready to throw himself out of the way of stray bullets.

At the bar, he saw Gates' other two companions straighten up, their hands perilously close to their guns. Alby Pearson was seated to Battles' right, and since the man was left-handed, this placed his gun right next to Battles.

"Gates," Parmalee said, "I'm giving you a chance—"

"You got a decision, my friend," Gates said. "Either pay me back the money you took from me by cheatin', go for your gun, or get up right now and walk out of here."

"Well," Parmalee said, "I guess you don't give me much choice. I can't give you back the money you lost, because then you wouldn't learn a lesson from it. I also can't get up and walk out. For one thing, I'm not so sure you wouldn't just shoot me in the back."

"I ain't no backshooter!"

"Maybe not, but what about your friends?"

"What?"

"You got three men backing your play, Gates," Parmalee said. "You tell me which one of us is the coward."

"Why you—"

Gates went for his gun, but he was slow. Pearson pushed back from the table to reach for his gun, but he was even slower.

Parmalee gripped the edge of the table and up-ended it toward Gates. That knocked the big man over onto his back, and it also shielded Parmalee from the two men at the bar, who were drawing their guns.

As Pearson's hand closed on his gun, Charlie Battles' hand fell on top of it, pinning it there. In his other hand Battles held a small derringer pointed at Pearson's head.

"Don't" was all Battles said, but it was enough.

Parmalee shifted to a wider grip on the table. He set his legs, and then lifted the table and rushed toward the bar with it. The two men, guns out, didn't know what to do, and before they could decide, Parmalee had thrown the table at them. They both reached out to catch it, but it slammed into them, knocking one gun loose.

Parmalee came in behind the table and took hold of the wrist of the man who was still holding his gun. Parmalee's large, powerful hand squeezed, and small bones rubbed together and then cracked. The man screamed, released his gun and fell to his knees.

Parmalee turned to face the other man, who was looking around on the floor for his gun. He took two steps, grabbed the man by the front of the shirt and drove his fist into his face. When he released his hold on the shirt, the man dropped to the floor.

He turned to look at Gates, who was picking himself up off the floor. Gates' gun was still in its holster, and as he spotted Parmalee, he started to reach for it. Parmalee rushed the man, driving into him with all of his weight. They both went down to the floor together, Gates grunting aloud as they landed. Parmalee's fall was padded by Gates, and he rolled off the man and snatched Gates' gun from his holster.

He stood up and looked down at Gates.

"I said no guns," he said, and tossed Gates' gun aside. "Get up!"

Gates glared up at Parmalee, then looked around at all of the people who were watching them. To save face, he had to get up and fight Parmalee.

Parmalee waited while Gates got to his feet and faced him.

"Now you've got some choices," Parmalee

said. "You can apologize and then turn and walk out, or we can fight. Personally, I'd rather you walked out. I don't want to have to hurt you."

Gates looked around the room nervously, and Parmalee knew what he was thinking.

"Don't let all of these people make your decision for you, Gates. You're all alone now, with no one to back you up. The smart thing would be to cut your losses and walk away."

"I had money on the table," Gates said grudgingly.

Parmalee looked down at the floor and saw some money at his feet. He bent and picked up a few dollars, walked to Gates and handed it to him.

"Now get out."

"I had more—"

"Gates . . ."

Gates tried to match Parmalee's stare, but all the bluster had gone out of the man.

"What's going on here?" a new voice asked.

Parmalee looked over at the batwing doors and saw a man with a badge standing just inside. Beyond the man, he thought he saw a child's face staring into the saloon from beneath the doors, but he wasn't sure.

"We're just finishing up a poker game, Sheriff," Parmalee said.

The sheriff looked past Parmalee and said, "Charlie, you in on this?"

"Like the man said, Sheriff," Battles said, putting his derringer away, "we're just finishing up a game."

"Take your friends with you, Gates," Parmalee said.

Charlie Battles nudged Alby Pearson, who got up off his chair and went to the bar to help the other two men up. The three of them then walked over to Gates and followed him past the sheriff and out of the saloon.

"All right," the sheriff said, "looks like the excitement is all over. Everybody go back to what you were doing before. Charlie? Can I get an explanation from you?"

"Sure, Sheriff," Charlie said. Battles looked around and said to some nearby men, "Could we get some help gettin' this money off the floor?"

"Sure, Charlie," someone said, and then a few men started picking it all up.

"Get a drink on me," Battles said to Parmalee, "and we'll settle up after I talk to the sheriff."

Parmalee nodded, and stepped up to the bar.

Outside the saloon Joey Shea was excited. She was very impressed with the big man she had heard someone call "Parmalee." If she could get Parmalee to come to work for her father, then she wouldn't be in trouble when she went home tonight.

She decided that she would wait as long as she had to for Parmalee to come out of the saloon.

CHAPTER TWO

While Parmalee was standing at the bar, a man approached with a smile fixed on his face.

"You handled that very well," the man said. "I want to thank you."

"Who are you?"

"Nick Abel."

Abel was tall and very thin, with snow-white hair. He was probably about fifty.

"Thank me for what?"

"For handling the situation with a minimum of breakage and bloodshed. You could just as easily have used your gun."

"Using a gun is never easy."

"Not when you're our age," Abel said. He either thought Parmalee was closer to fifty than forty, or he was closer to forty than fifty. Parmalee took a look in the mirror and decided it was the latter. "When you're younger, it always seems the easiest thing to do."

Parmalee stared at Abel and ran the name around in his head. He didn't remember the man ever having a rep as a gunhand, but maybe he got smart very young. It had taken Parmalee a while, but he had finally come to the same conclusion. Now he drew his gun only when he absolutely had no other choice.

"Any truth to the four bits story?" Parmalee asked.

Abel seemed a little surprised at the question, but then said, "That depends on how you heard it."

Parmalee told Abel what he had heard, and the man nodded.

"That's the truth, all right."

"Sounds like hard work."

Abel grinned. "The hard part was getting them to let me in the game with only four bits. After that it was just a matter of wearing the bastards down."

After talking with the sheriff, Charlie Battles had returned and was approaching the bar.

"Here's the money, Charlie," a man said, and handed Battles two handfuls.

"Thanks, Ethan."

Battles came to the bar and deposited the money on top of it.

"Take out what's yours," he said to Parmalee, then turned to the bartender. "A beer, Al."

"Comin' up."

Parmalee counted out his money and pocketed it.

"I see you've met the boss," Battles said over his beer mug.

"Your drinks are on me, by the way," Abel said.

"Much obliged," Parmalee said.

"Well, have another," Battles said to Parmalee, " 'cause I promised you one."

Parmalee looked at the bartender, who brought him another beer.

"The rest of that money all yours?" Nick Abel asked Battles.

"That other fella's got some coming, too," Parmalee said.

"That'd be Dave Myers," Battles said. "I'll take out what's comin' to me, and we'll give him the rest. He was playin' about even, I think, but now he'll be coming out ahead."

"I'm sure he won't mind," Parmalee said. "Everything straightened out with the sheriff?"

"Oh, sure," Battles said. "Sheriff Whitley and I are friends. He listened to what I had to say."

"Charlie here is sort of Ken Whitley's third deputy," Abel said to Parmalee.

"When he needs one," Battles added.

"Glad you were in the game, then," Parmalee said.

"Oh, I wouldn't have pressed charges against you, Mr. . . ."

"Parmalee."

"Mr. Parmalee," Abel said. "As I said, the breakage was minimal. What's a table and a couple of chairs?"

"Appreciate it," Parmalee said.

"If you gentlemen would excuse me, I've got some work to do. If there's anything else I can do for you, Mr. Parmalee—something to eat; a girl, maybe—just let me know. We like to show strangers good hospitality."

"I'll keep it in mind."

Abel nodded to both of them and left.

"Pick out a girl, Parmalee," Battles said. "It ain't often Abel offers one of his girls for free."

Parmalee looked around at the four or five girls who were working the room. They all had something to recommend them. Two of them were blond, one short and busty, the other tall, long-legged. Two of them had dark hair—one wore it long and the other real short—and there was one redhead with pale skin and freckles on the slopes of her breasts. They all looked like they were between twenty and thirty years old.

"I think I'll pass," he said finally.

"Well, don't take him up on his offer to eat," Battles warned. "The food here is terrible."

"I am sort of hungry."

"If you'll have dinner with me, I can make sure you get a decent steak."

"Sounds good."

"Finish your beer," Battles said, setting his own empty mug on the bar. "The cafe is just down the block."

"Joey, what are you doin' here?"

Joey turned around and looked up at Sheriff Ken Whitley.

"Hello, Sheriff."

"Do your parents know you're in town this late?"

"Uh, well—"

"Your hide's gonna be tanned good when you get home," the sheriff said.

"Yes, sir."

"Then get on home and take your whippin'," Whitley said.

Joey got up from her knees, where she had still been peering into the saloon beneath the batwing doors, and faced the sheriff.

"Yes, sir."

"Git!"

She ran from the saloon then, but she was still determined to get Parmalee to work for her pa. She'd just have to wait for tomorrow to ask him— that is, if she was still able to walk by then, *and* if she was even allowed out of her room.

Battles had been right about the steak. Parmalee had enjoyed it so much that he asked for another one.

"You have a large appetite," the waitress commented. She was fortyish, and had been giving Parmalee special attention all night. He, on the other hand, was not paying her any mind at all, except when he wanted another steak, or more coffee.

"You had yourself quite a reputation a few years ago, didn't you?" Battles asked during dinner.

"Did I?" Parmalee asked without looking at the man.

"You sure did," Battles said, "then all of a sudden you sort of disappeared."

"I didn't disappear," Parmalee said. "I stopped killing people. When you're killing people, you tend to get noticed. When you stop. . . ." He finished the sentence with a shrug.

It wasn't just a few years ago that he had stopped; it was more like nine. At thirty-two, he had suddenly decided that he didn't want to be a gun for hire for the rest of his life. People rarely looked at him; it was his gun they were interested in. It wasn't he who was holding the gun, but the other way around. He was just a body at the ass end of a gun, and he didn't want to be that forever.

"Why'd you stop?"

Parmalee looked at Battles this time.

"That isn't the question you should be asking," Parmalee said. He pushed away the plate with the remains of his first steak and stood up. "Everybody always asks the wrong question."

"Parmalee . . ." Battles said, but then the man decided he wouldn't be able to get Parmalee to sit back down again. "All right, so what's the right question?"

"What you should ask," Parmalee said, "and what everyone else should ask, is why I started."

Parmalee started to walk away when the waitress came with his second steak.

"Hey, what about your other steak?"

"He's paying for it," he said, without looking back, "let him eat it."

CHAPTER THREE

When Joey Shea entered town the next morning, she figured she'd try the hotels looking for Parmalee. She'd gotten a good hide tanning last night when she got home, and was told not to leave her room today. At eight A.M., she opened her window, slipped out, and walked to town. It was a two-mile-long walk that she had made many times before, in daylight and at night. She still figured that if she could get Parmalee to work for her father, her parents would forgive her everything. Maybe they'd even stop fighting with each other.

She was approaching the Culverton House Hotel when she saw Parmalee come walking out. She could have approached him right there, but she decided to wait until he went somewhere for breakfast and got off the street.

Parmalee didn't know where to go for breakfast, so he decided to go to the same cafe he and

Battles had eaten at the night before. At least this time he'd be eating alone. That's what he should have done the night before. If Battles thought he was entitled to the story of Parmalee's life just for a steak, he was more wrong than he knew.

There was a different waitress working this morning, and that suited Parmalee, too. When he was eating, he didn't want some woman hanging around him, trying to make an impression. This one was fat and fifty and bored. He ordered steak and eggs, biscuits and coffee, and told her to bring the coffee right away.

While he was working on his second cup, a little girl walked up to his table, pulled out the other chair and sat down. At least, he thought it was a little girl. She had short blond hair and a dirt-smudged face and could have been a boy, but he doubted it.

He looked around for her parents, but the other two tables were taken by men, and neither seemed interested in her.

"You lost, kid?" he asked.

"No."

"What are you doing here?"

"Your name Parmalee?"

"That's right."

"I wanna talk to you."

"About what?"

"A job."

"What kind of job."

"Workin' for my father."

"Who's your father?"

"His name's Ted Shea. My name's Joey."

"Joey?"

She made a face and said, "Josephine."

"Look, kid—"

"My pa can pay you—"

"I'm not interested in a job—"

"Won't you just talk to my father? He needs help."

The waitress came with his breakfast and set it down in front of him. "Anything for her?" she asked.

"Yeah—" Joey said, but Parmalee cut her off.

"No," he said, "she's not eating."

"That's no way to treat your kid," the waitress said, and walked away before Parmalee could correct her.

"I'm hungry," Joey said.

"Go home and eat."

"I can't go home," she insisted, "not without you."

"Why not?"

"I'm not even supposed to be out of my room," she said. "I'll get my hide tanned for this, again."

"Again?"

She nodded. "Got tanned last night 'cause I was in town. I saw what happened in the saloon. You just gotta help my pa."

"What's your father do?"

"We got us a ranch a couple of miles out of town, and we got to drive some cattle to Kansas."

"I'm not a drover."

"It's not a big herd, but it's what my pa's got. He don't need someone to help him drive them; he needs protection."

"From who?"

"From my grandpa Max."

"Your grandfather wants to stop your father?"

"Yes."

"Why?"

"I don't understand why," she said. "It's grown-up stuff. But my pa can tell you why if you'll come home with me."

"Look, kid," Parmalee said, "all I want to do now is eat my breakfast. This just doesn't sound like my kind of job, okay?"

"You won't help?"

"No."

"Mister—"

"Good-bye, kid," he said. "I'd like to eat my breakfast in peace."

She glared at him and said, "You're a mean man."

He didn't answer. She stared at him for a few moments, then slid off the chair and walked out the door.

"Hey, mister," the waitress said, "was that your kid?"

"No!"

She stared at him a moment, then shrugged her beefy shoulders and decided not to try and figure it out. She had heard what the little girl called him, a "mean man." He sure had the looks of one.

"Where's Joey?" Ted Shea asked.

"Damned if I know," Laura Shea replied.

"Laura, you're her mother."

Laura Shea, dark-haired and pretty, looked up from her sewing at her husband and said, "That don't mean I know where she is every minute of every day."

Ted Shea had been out early, checking the herd. It wasn't a good idea to let them go untended for too long. In fact, he had come back to the house to get Joey so that she could keep an eye on them while he went into town.

"She's supposed to be in her room," Ted Shea said. "Didn't I tell her to stay in her room, after what happened last night?"

"You told her," Laura said, "but I'll bet she was out the window at first light."

"If you knew that, why didn't you say something?"

Laura looked at him again. "Come on, Ted," she said, "you knew it, too. You know damn well that girl does what she pleases no matter how many times you tan her hide."

"Do you have to curse?" Ted said. "I don't want her learning it."

"Yes, dear," Laura said, and looked back to her sewing. The sarcasm in her tone did not escape her husband.

When, Ted Shea wondered, had things gotten so bad? He was sure Laura didn't love him anymore, and recently it was looking like Joey was going to be just like her mother. She was blond, like her father, but after that the resemblance faded. She was becoming more and more like her mother, stubborn and contrary.

When Ted had married Max Venable's daughter twelve years ago, they had been so in love. Or maybe they had just gotten married to spite old Max. Maybe that was it.

"I'm going to town," Ted said.

"You'll probably find your daughter there,"

Laura said without looking up. "She probably went looking for that man she told us about last night."

"I've told her so many times not to go talking to strangers—" He stopped short and looked at his wife. "If it's not too much trouble, you can take a look at the herd from time to time until I get back."

"If Max wants the herd, he can just come and take it," she said. She had been calling her father "Max" ever since she was married.

"He doesn't want to take it," Ted pointed out, "he wants us to lose it."

"Take it, lose it, it's all the same," she said wearily. "Either way, Max wins."

"Max is not going to win," he said tightly. "Now, while I'm gone, you check on the herd, understand?"

"I understand, Ted," she said. "I understand perfectly."

Ted Shea left his house, wishing he could say the same thing.

CHAPTER FOUR

After leaving Parmalee in the cafe, Joey Shea
walked across the street, sat down on the boardwalk and rested her chin on the heels of her
hands. She wasn't about to give up on trying to
get Parmalee to work for her father. She just had
to figure out a way to convince him. She had
given him her best "poor little girl" look, and it
hadn't worked. It was plain to Joey that Parmalee
was not only a mean man, but a hard one. She had
heard men like Parmalee called "cold," and she
thought the term fitted him very nicely.

Joey was still trying to figure out a way when
she saw her father riding down the street toward
her. It occurred to her to run, but it was too late
for that. She might as well face him and take her
punishment.

She stood up as her father directed his horse to
approach her.

"Josephine Shea," Ted Shea said.

"Yes, Pa."

Ted stopped his horse and dismounted. "What did I tell you last night, young lady?"

"Pa, I know what you told me, but—"

"Never mind 'but,'" he said harshly. "Don't you get tired of having your hide tanned?"

"Pa, I was just tryin' to help—"

"Help? I needed you to help me this morning, young lady, and you were nowhere to be found. Why do you think you can just run off whenever you feel like it?"

"Pa, I didn't just run off, I came to talk to Parmalee—"

"That man again? I told you before, you're not supposed to talk to strangers—"

"But he can help you. All you have to do is get him to work for you."

"And how am I supposed to do that?"

"Talk to him," she said. "He's across the street having breakfast."

In spite of himself, Ted Shea found himself looking across the street. Then he looked farther down the street on his side and saw the sheriff's office.

"Come with me," he said to Joey.

"Where are we goin'?"

"To the sheriff's office."

She swallowed hard. "You're not gonna put me in jail for not obeying you, are you, Pa?"

It occurred to Ted Shea to let her go on thinking that for a little while, but he had to smile at the look on her face and the tone in her voice when she asked.

"No, Joey," he said, "I'm not gonna let him put

you in jail. I'm gonna ask the sheriff some questions about this man Parmalee."

"Then you are gonna try and hire Parmalee?"

He patted her on the shoulder and said, "Let's talk to the sheriff first."

"Ain't that the old man's son-in-law?" Harry Pringle asked.

The other man with him, Chris Lake, said, "Yeah, it sure is."

"What do you say we go over and spook him a little?"

"I don't know," Lake hesitated. "He's got his daughter with him. The old man don't want nothin' happenin' to his granddaughter."

"We won't touch the little girl," Pringle said. "Come on, we'll have us some fun."

Pringle stepped off the boardwalk, and Lake reluctantly followed.

When Parmalee came out of the cafe, he saw the little girl across the street with her father. They were walking toward the sheriff's office. Farther down the street, on his side, he saw two men—one of whom was huge—also watching the girl and her father. There was a predatory cast to the way the men were watching and standing, especially the big one. They looked as if they were ready to cross the street until they stopped short, realizing where the man and little girl were headed.

Parmalee looked around him, found a hard-backed wooden chair against the front of the cafe, and sat down to watch, just for want of something better to do.

* * *

Pringle pressed a massive paw to Lake's chest and said, "We'll get 'em when they come out of the sheriff's office."

"Maybe we should just forget—" Lake began, but he stopped when Pringle's powerful hand closed on his shoulder. Lake's arm suddenly went numb.

"We'll wait," Pringle said.

"Sure, Harry," Lake gasped, "whatever you say."

"What do you know about Parmalee?" Ted Shea asked Sheriff Whitley.

"Did this little one get her hide tanned last night?" Whitley asked, looking down at Joey.

"Yes, she did," Ted said, "and probably will again today. Kevin, what do you know about Parmalee?"

At forty-one, Whitley was six years older than Ted Shea. They had both grown up in this town. At one time both had worked for Max Venable. For the past twelve years, Ted had been on his own. Sheriff Kevin Whitley, however, was not only still working for Venable, but since he had become sheriff five years ago, he was also in Venable's pocket. He may have been wearing the sheriff's badge, but the tin star was owned by Max Venable.

"Why are you interested, Ted?" Whitley asked.

"I just am."

"Still lookin' for someone to drive that herd with you?"

"What do you think?"

"I don't think the old man would like it if you hired Parmalee."

Ted poked Whitley in the chest with his fore-finger and said, "You just gave me a good enough reason to do it, Kevin."

"Don't try it, Ted."

"Why not?"

"Parmalee's just not the kind of man you want to mess with."

"What's wrong with him?"

"He's a killer, pure and simple. A cold-blooded killer."

"Work for money, does he?"

"He used to. I hear he doesn't hire his gun out much anymore."

"Well, I don't want to hire his gun," Ted said. "All I want is a man who won't spook."

"Well, Parmalee won't spook, I can tell you that," Whitley said.

"Not even by the old man?"

Whitley hesitated, then said, "That'd be inter-estin' to see."

"You may have the chance," Ted said. "Come on, Joey. Let's go."

"I'd be careful if I was you, Ted."

"I'll keep that in mind, Kevin."

Outside the office, Joey asked, "Are you gonna talk to him, Pa? Are you gonna talk to Parmalee?"

Ted Shea looked down at his daughter and was struck by how much she looked like her mother— or looked the way her mother must have looked at the same age.

"I'm gonna try, honey," he said, stroking her head. "I'm gonna try."

* * *

"There they are," Pringle said. "Let's go."

"Harry, this may not be such a good idea—"

Pringle's hand closed on Lake's upper arm, and he said, "Let's go, Chris."

"I'm with you, Harry."

CHAPTER FIVE

Parmalee watched as the situation developed, and he certainly had no intention of stepping in. He had learned a long time ago to mind his own business—but that didn't mean he couldn't watch.

Ted Shea and his daughter crossed the street and mounted the boardwalk. Their intention was to walk down toward the cafe to see if Parmalee was there. No sooner had they mounted the walk, than their path was blocked by two men.

"Pa—" Joey said, gripping her father's hand.

"Easy, Joey," Ted said. "If there's trouble, you run, you hear?"

"For the sheriff?"

"Just run, honey," he said. "These men work for your grandfather, and so does the sheriff. You just run someplace safe, hear?"

"I hear, Pa."

The Sheas kept walking until their path was directly blocked. One man was huge, almost six and a half feet tall, with wide shoulders, a thick chest and waist, and legs like tree trunks. The other man was not small, standing six feet, but he was slender, and dwarfed by his partner.

"Ted Shea, ain't it?" the big man said.

"That's right."

"You know who I work for, Shea?"

"I know."

"Old Max, you ain't one of his favorite people, you know?"

"That breaks my heart."

"And if he don't like you," Pringle said, poking Ted in the chest with a finger like a railroad spike, "that means I don't like you."

"That breaks my heart even more."

"It can break more than that," Pringle said, "like your back."

"Harry," Lake warned, "the little girl. . . ."

"My partner here is worried about your little girl," Pringle said. "Why don't you send her on her way so's we can finish our business."

"We don't have any business . . . what's your name?"

"Pringle."

Joey shivered. She had heard stories about this man Pringle.

"I don't have any business with you, Pringle, so stand aside."

"Stand aside," Pringle repeated. He looked at Lake and said, "Stand aside, he says."

Lake shrugged.

"You gonna use that gun on me, farmer?" Pringle asked.

"Not unless you force me to," Ted said. "I'm no gunman."

"Neither am I," Pringle said. "Whataya say we settle our differences with our hands, huh?"

"Pa—" Joey said warningly.

"Be still, Joey," Ted said without looking at her. "Pringle, I got no quarrel with you—"

Pringle's hand came out and slammed into Ted's chest, knocking him back several feet—and it wasn't even that hard a shove!

"I say you do."

"Joey," Ted said, "get goin'."

"But Pa—"

"Move, Joey!"

"Go on, little girl," Pringle said, smiling down at her. Joey's eyes widened as she looked into the big man's eyes. "Go on, you don't want to see your pa's back broken, do you?"

"Joey . . . go!" With that, Ted Shea stepped in and hit Pringle in the face with his fist as hard as he could. Pringle grunted, and then a smile spread slowly across his face.

"Now you dunnit, farmer," he said.

Joey started to run, but stopped halfway across the street. She didn't know where to go.

She turned and saw Pringle hit her father, knocking him back a few feet, and then down. Pringle followed the fallen man and kicked him, knocking him into the street.

"Go on!" Pringle said to Lake, and Lake stepped into the street and gave Ted Shea a kick of his own.

"Pa," Joey said, her eyes filling with tears.

She looked around, thought about going to the

sheriff's office in spite of what her pa said, and that's when she saw Parmalee sitting against the front of the cafe, watching. She ran toward him.

"Parmalee, you got to help my pa!" she cried.

"I do?" he asked. "I told you, I ain't interested in working for your pa."

"But . . . but they're gonna kill him."

"A man's got to learn how to take care of himself."

"But . . . there's two of them."

"Go and get the sheriff," Parmalee told her.

"I can't! They work for my grandfather, and so does the sheriff."

"The sheriff works for the town, little girl."

"This one works for my grandfather. He won't help my pa."

At that moment the door to the sheriff's office opened, and the sheriff Parmalee had seen the night before stepped out onto the walk. That was as far as he went, though. He remained where he was and watched as the two men continued to beat and kick Joey Shea's father.

"Your grandfather, is he a rich man?"

"Yes."

"Folks around here scared of him?"

"Yes."

Parmalee made a face and said "Shit" beneath his breath. Years ago Parmalee had worked for men like that, selling them his gun. Now he hated men like that and took every opportunity he could to make their lives as complicated as he could.

He got up from the chair and told the girl, "Stay here."

He started walking down the street toward the

three men. When he reached them, the smaller assailant was holding Joey Shea's father up while the larger man pounded him. By now there were people watching from both sides of the street, but no one was stepping in to help.

"That's enough," Parmalee said.

The two men didn't hear him.

"I said . . . that's enough!" Parmalee shouted.

Now the two men stopped, and Pringle turned around to look at him.

"You talkin' to us?" the big man asked.

"Let him go," Parmalee said.

"What's it to you?"

"You're scarin' his little girl."

Pringle grinned. "Really?"

Parmalee looked past Pringle to Lake and said, "Let him go."

Chris Lake looked into Parmalee's eyes and released Ted Shea, who fell to his knees.

"Friend, you better move along," Pringle said. "This ain't none of your business."

"The little girl asked for my help," Parmalee said. "That makes it my business."

Pringle turned to face Parmalee and asked, "You gonna use that gun on me?"

"That's up to you."

"I tell you what," Pringle said, grinning, "why don't we just settle this man to man?"

"Sure."

Pringle's grin widened, and he took one step toward Parmalee. Parmalee immediately drew his gun and shot the big man in the right knee. Pringle stopped, staggered, and a look of shock and pain came over his face.

"Wha—" Pringle bent over to clutch at his knee and looked up at Parmalee.

"Just giving myself an edge," Parmalee said, holstering the gun. He stepped in and hit Pringle in the face. The man's wounded knee would not hold him, and he fell over onto his side. The punch hadn't hurt him much, but he made no effort to get up.

Parmalee looked at the other man and said, "What about you?"

"I got no beef with you, mister," Chris Lake said, moving away from Ted Shea.

"Better get your friend to the doctor, then."

Lake nodded, moved around Ted Shea while keeping a wary eye on Parmalee, and helped Pringle stagger to his feet. The big man dragged his wounded leg as Lake helped him move away.

Joey Shea ran over to her father and threw her arms around his neck.

"Pa, are you all right?"

"I'll be fine, honey," Ted said. He was bleeding from the nose, and from a cut over his eye, but he didn't seem to be seriously hurt. He looked up at Parmalee and said, "Thanks for your help."

Parmalee took out his gun, ejected the empty shell and shoved in a live one. That done, he holstered his gun, and then looked over at the sheriff, who was still watching.

"You got a problem with what happened here?" he asked the lawman.

The sheriff didn't answer; he just turned, went back into his office, and closed the door.

CHAPTER SIX

Parmalee helped Ted Shea to his feet and walked him over to the cafe. The same waitress watched them come in, surprised to see Parmalee with the little girl again, and another man. When she recognized the man as Ted Shea, she realized that the girl was *his* daughter, Josephine. She hadn't recognized her earlier.

Parmalee dropped Ted into a chair and told the waitress, "Coffee."

"What happened to him?"

"Just bring some coffee," Parmalee said, and the waitress retreated.

Joey sat down next to her father, and Parmalee sat across from both of them.

"I understand Joey asked you for some help for us and you refused," Ted said.

"That's right."

"Why did you help me out there, then?"

"Joey told me that her grandfather is rich and powerful."

"That's right, he is."

"Is this your father?"

Ted shook his head. "Father-in-law. Are you hoping to get some money out of him? Because if you are, you're going about it the wrong way. He's certainly not going to reward you for this."

"No, that's not it," Parmalee said. "I just have a dislike for men like that, men with money who think they can do anything they want."

"That's Max."

"Max?"

"Max Venable. If you've ever been around here before, you'll know the name."

"No, I've never been here before," Parmalee said. "I'm just passing through."

"Did Joey tell you why I need help?"

"Something about driving a herd."

"To a Kansas railhead. From there I'll ship them to Texas. I need the money from this sale to survive, otherwise Max Venable will get what he wants."

"And what's that?"

"My failure. He's hoping that my wife, Laura, will leave me and go to live with him, with Joey."

"I ain't gonna live with Grandpa," Joey said.

"Hush," her father said.

The waitress came with a pot of coffee then, set it down and again retreated from Parmalee's gaze. Joey poured her father a cup of coffee. Parmalee poured one for himself.

"I can't pay you much," Ted continued.

"Mr. Shea, how many hands do you have for this drive now?"

"None."

"None?"

"It's not a big herd, Mr. Parmalee," Ted said. "Two men could handle it."

"And me, I can help," Joey added.

Ted smiled and said, "She can, too. She's a very good rider."

"Two men and a kid," Parmalee said.

"And my ma," Joey said, "but she ain't much help when it comes to work."

"My wife will do the cooking. The drive won't take as long as some of the bigger ones. I figure it should take us about—"

"Mr. Shea, wait," Parmalee said, holding up his hand. "I haven't said I'll work for you."

"But . . . what you did out there."

"What I did out there I did for a reason," Parmalee said. "From what you tell me, your father-in-law isn't just going to sit back and watch you drive your herd to Kansas. He's going to try to stop you."

"Not outright," Ted said, "but he will try to make it as difficult on us as he can—not that it won't be hard enough without him."

"I really can't see tying myself down to something like this for weeks. . . . I'm sorry, but I can't come to work for you."

"I see," Ted said, looking down at his coffee cup. He drank the remaining liquid and set it down. "Well, thank you for what you did out on the street. I appreciate it. Joey? I got some business at the bank, and then we'll go on home."

"Am I gonna get tanned?" Joey asked.

Ted Shea smiled and said, "No, I don't think so. Not this time."

Ted and Joey Shea stood up and walked out without further words to or from Parmalee, who poured himself another cup of coffee.

"What happened?" Rex Cameron asked. Cameron was the foreman of Max Venable's ranch. Right now he was at the doctor's office with Pringle and Lake.

"Ted Shea's gunman shot me in the knee," Pringle said. He looked at Lake, daring the man to contradict him.

"Lake?"

"That's what happened, Rex," Lake said.

"Looks like Shea's hired a gun to fight the old man," Pringle said.

"Do you know who the man was?" Cameron asked.

"No," Pringle said, wincing as the doctor worked on his knee. "I didn't know 'im."

"This knee isn't going to be much good for anything in the future," the doctor said. "Your leg will probably be stiff from now on."

"I won't be able to work?" Pringle asked.

"Not as a cowhand," the doctor said.

"That son of a bitch!" Pringle said. "He didn't have to do this."

"Lake, get Pringle back to the ranch. I'm gonna talk to the sheriff about this."

"The sheriff," Pringle said with distaste. "All he did was watch."

"Get him home," Cameron said to Lake again.

"Right."

Cameron left the office and stopped outside, where two more of his men were waiting.

"Is Harry gonna be all right?" Larry Crews asked.

"He ain't ever gonna walk right again," Cameron said. "I'm goin' over to the sheriff's office. I'll meet you fellas in front of the general store. Help Lake get Pringle up onto a horse."

"Right," Carl Martin said. "Are we goin' after the man who shot Harry?"

Cameron gave the man a look and said, "Not without finding out who we're up against first."

When Rex Cameron entered the sheriff's office, Kevin Whitley knew what was coming.

"Rex."

"Tell me about it, Kevin," Cameron said, "and don't leave anythin' out."

"About what?"

"Ted Shea's gunman."

"What?"

"The man who shot Pringle."

"Parmalee."

Cameron frowned. "Dan Parmalee?"

"That's him."

"He's workin' for Shea?"

"Not that I know of."

"Didn't he shoot Pringle?"

"Sure he did, but he wasn't workin' for Shea."

"Pringle said he was."

"Pringle's a liar. He and Lake decided to kick

Shea around some, and Parmalee stepped in. That's about all I know."

"How do you know Parmalee's not working for Shea?" Cameron asked.

"He wasn't before that happened," Whitley said. "Shea was in here just minutes before, asking me about Parmalee like you are now. Wanted to know who he was."

"Then maybe he hired him after he left here."

"Might have, but I don't think he had time."

"Why would Parmalee take a hand if he wasn't working for Shea?"

"Maybe he just didn't like seein' two men beat up on one," Whitley suggested, "or maybe he did it for the little girl."

"The old man's granddaughter was there?"

"She sure was."

"Son of a bitch," Cameron swore under his breath. He hated to fire Pringle after the man had taken a bullet, but if he had started trouble with Shea while the girl, Joey, was around, he was going to have to. In fact, he'd have to try and keep the old man from killing Pringle.

"All right," Cameron said, "all right. Why didn't you stop it?"

"Stop which? Pringle and Lake work for the old man. I wasn't about to step in on them."

"And Parmalee?"

Whitley laughed. "You think I get paid enough to go up against the likes of Parmalee?"

"No," Cameron said, "I guess not."

"You're damned right not."

"Okay," Cameron said, "I'll explain it all to Mr. Venable."

Cameron left the sheriff's office, a worried frown on his face. If Ted Shea had Dan Parmalee working for him, Max Venable wasn't going to like it one bit.

CHAPTER SEVEN

When Cameron returned to Max Venable's ranch, Pringle was already resting on his bunk in the bunkhouse. The foreman decided to talk to Venable before firing Pringle. He found his boss in his office, which was one of thirteen rooms in the huge house he had built, largely with his own hands.

"You look like you've got something on your mind," Venable said, looking up from his desk. Cameron had been working for Venable for fifteen years, and Venable had secretly hoped that Cameron and his daughter would marry. That was just one more thing he held against Ted Shea.

Venable was a tall man whose height was giving way to his age. Once he stood proudly and erect at six-two, but now he was bent over slightly, as if the weight of his years were eroding his height. He had always been slender, but now he was painfully thin, another concession to his sixty-eight years. Still and all, he was as healthy as a bull, according to his doctor, and could look forward to at least another twenty years of life.

Cameron closed the door to the office, and Venable frowned.

"What's wrong?" Venable asked.

"It looks like your son-in-law has hired himself a professional gun."

"What?" There was naked disbelief on Venable's face. "Who?"

"Dan Parmalee."

"Parmalee," Venable repeated. "That name is familiar."

"He was much more active ten or more years ago," Cameron said. "Fact is, I thought he was retired, or dead."

"Did you see him?"

"No, but Pringle and Lake did. He shot Pringle in the knee."

Venable sat back in his chair with a sigh. "Tell me about it."

Cameron told his boss the whole story, including the fact that his granddaughter was on the scene.

"Shot in the knee, you say?"

"That's right."

"Should have killed the bastard," Venable said. "I'd give him a raise if it wasn't for the fact that Joey was there. Fire him!"

"Yes, sir."

"He's lucky I don't kill him myself."

"I'll tell him."

"No, tell him he's fired because he couldn't handle Parmalee."

"Why?"

"Maybe he'll go after him again, stiff leg and all."

"Wouldn't stand much of a chance alone and crippled."

"Who was with him?"

"Lake."

"Fire him, too. Same reason."

"Yes, sir."

Max Venable rubbed his jaw with the long, skinny fingers of his left hand. His knuckles seemed too large for his hands.

"Pick out five men and have them go into town without guns."

"What for?"

"I want them to take this Parmalee out of the picture," the old man said.

"He'll kill them."

"Not if they're unarmed."

"You're betting that he won't shoot an unarmed man."

"That's right."

"You're betting their lives."

"Give them a raise," Venable said. "Any man who won't do it is fired. We got some mean sons of bitches on this ranch. Give them the job."

"You want him dead?"

"Takes a lot to beat a man to death," Venable said. "I know, I did it once. Wasn't the same for a week. No, they can cripple him, maybe lay him up so that he can't work for my son-in-law until it's too late."

"I'll see to it."

"Not personally," Venable said. "I don't want

you anywhere near town when they do it. Just make sure it's taken care of."

"All right," Cameron said. "Should I say anythin' to the sheriff?"

"He'll stay out of the way."

A few moments of silence followed, as if each man was waiting for the other to say something, and then Max Venable said, "Anything else?"

"No, sir."

"That's all, then."

"Yes, sir," Cameron said, and started for the door.

"Rex?"

"Yes, sir?"

"Thanks for staying on top of things."

Cameron smiled. "That's my job."

The foreman left, and Max Venable thought about his granddaughter. He hadn't seen her in months, and that had only been a glance in town. Even that day he'd managed to get into an argument with her father, and Joey had run from him. He loved his granddaughter, even more than he did his daughter. He wanted Laura and Joey to come and live with him, but if he could, he'd take Joey from her parents and be happy.

He thought about Dan Parmalee. He remembered him now, from years ago. What had he been doing for the past eight or ten years, and why was he now working for Ted Shea? How could Ted Shea even pay a man like Parmalee?

Well, whatever the reason, Dan Parmalee would soon find out what folly it was to go up against Max Venable.

* * *

Before he even left the house, Rex Cameron had the five men picked out in his mind. If Harry Pringle hadn't already made the mistake of tangling with Parmalee, he would have been one of them. Now he and Chris Lake would be off Venable land by nightfall, and hopefully, Parmalee would be unable to even stand, let alone work for Ted Shea.

Cameron thought about Laura Shea. Twelve years ago she had been a stunning beauty. Now, after years of needless hardships, she was still a handsome woman, and he loved her no less. Not even Max Venable knew that Rex Cameron had loved Laura back then, and still did.

That was the foreman's secret.

CHAPTER EIGHT

Parmalee had been in town one full day, and already he had been involved in a bar fight, a street fight, and he had shot one man. He had also turned down an offer of a job from a little girl, and then her father. Twenty-four eventful hours, and yet, as he had dinner in that same cafe, he gave none of the principals in those incidents a second thought. After dinner he went back to the saloon without any worry that there might be another fight. The first one had not been his fault, anyway. He certainly wasn't going to stop winning at poker just because of one sore loser.

He approached the bar and ordered a beer. The bartender, the same one who had been working the night before, placed the full mug in front of him and leaned on the bar, as if he was going to say something. Parmalee beat him to it.

"You gonna watch me drink this?"

"Huh? Oh, uh, no, no. . . ."

The bartender drifted away, and Parmalee took a swallow of the cold beer. He turned to face the room, mug in hand, and looked around. The gaming tables were all in full swing, even though half the regular tables in the room were still empty. There was no one seated at the table where Parmalee had been playing the night before. Parmalee had no desire to play faro, blackjack or roulette. The only game that interested him was poker, and there was no house poker game in progress. Even if there was, he detested playing against the house.

While he worked on his beer, two of the girls—the leggy blonde and the short-haired brunette—came over and tried to "make friends." Parmalee told them he had all the friends he needed, and they pouted and moved away, feeling much colder for the encounter.

When the batwing doors opened and five men walked in, Parmalee sensed trouble. What he didn't know for sure was whether it was going to be directed at him or not. Given the way his first twenty-four hours had gone, though, it was more than likely.

He turned and beckoned to the bartender.

"You know those fellas?"

The bartender looked, then said, "Sure."

Parmalee waited a beat, then asked, "Well, who are they?"

"You want their names?"

"Just give me an idea, like where do they work?"

"That's easy," the bartender said, "they all work for Old Man Venable."

Parmalee nodded, and knew that trouble was headed his way.

"That's funny."

"What is?" Parmalee asked.

"They ain't wearin' guns," the bartender said. "None of them."

"I noticed that," Parmalee said. "Do they usually?"

"Sure do. It's funny, them not wearin' them tonight."

"Yeah," Parmalee said, "funny."

Now he knew what was coming. One or all of the men would pick a fight. If he shot one, he'd go to jail. If he didn't shoot any of them, they would beat him to a pulp—or try.

"What've you got behind the bar for trouble?" Parmalee asked.

"Huh?" The bartender actually looked under the bar and said, "Well, I got an over-and-under shotgun."

Parmalee shook his head. "Something less lethal."

"Well, I got an axe handle—"

"That'll do. Where is it?"

"Other end of the bar."

"Bring it down here and put it where I can reach it. Do it without anyone knowing what you're doing. Understand?"

"No," the bartender said, "but I'll do it."

Parmalee kept an eye on the men by using the mirror behind the bar while the bartender moved the axe handle.

"Do I have to send for the sheriff?" the bartender asked.

"What good would he do?" Parmalee asked. "He works for Venable, too, doesn't he?"

"You know a lot for somebody who's only been here a day."

"I'm a fast learner."

"Well, the axe handle is here."

"Okay," Parmalee said, "get lost."

"You got it."

The bartender moved down the bar as far away from Parmalee as he could.

The five men split into two groups. Two of them went to the roulette table, and the other three to a faro table. One played while two watched. The five of them took turns peering over their shoulders at Parmalee. He wondered how long he was going to have to wait before they made their move.

They came at him when he was halfway through his second beer.

The two from the roulette table approached first, on either side of him at the bar. During the past half hour, the saloon had filled up, but there was still plenty of room for them at the bar. Still, one of them banged into Parmalee's elbow, spilling beer from Parmalee's glass as well as his own.

"Goddamit!" the man roared. He was the biggest of the five, which was probably why he had been chosen to make the initial contact.

"Clumsy," Parmalee said.

"What?"

"I said that was clumsy."

"Are you calling me clumsy?"

"You hard of hearing as well as clumsy?" Parmalee asked. Might as well push it, he figured, get it over with.

"If you didn't have that gun—"

"We could get you one," Parmalee said, cutting the man off.

"What?"

"I said I'm sure someone here would loan you a gun, if we asked them real nice."

Parmalee turned and looked at the other man, who blinked and looked away.

"Your friend doesn't have one, and neither do your other friends."

"W-what other friends?"

"The mob you came in here with," Parmalee said. "Look, why don't we save some time here. You and your friends have been sent to beat up on me, right? And you figured if you came unarmed, I wouldn't use my gun. Right?"

"Whataya talkin' about?" the man said. "I came for a beer, and you spilled it. I'll take you on, but not with a gun; I ain't no gunhand."

"That's too bad."

A glance passed over Parmalee's shoulder, between the two men, and the first man shouted, "Grab 'im."

As the man behind him took hold of his arms, Parmalee reared back with his head. He felt the man's nose squash flat, and the hold on his arms loosened. He blocked a punch from the first man with his left and struck him on the chin with his right.

Without wasting time, he went for the axe handle, figuring that the other three men would be closing on him by now. As he turned back from the bar, axe handle in hand, he saw that they were almost on him. He swung the makeshift weapon and hit one of the men right across the face. The flesh over his cheek split open, and the man went down.

Parmalee put his back to the bar and grasped the axe handle with two hands, right in the center. He rushed forward and thrust both arms out ahead of him. The two remaining men were standing close enough together that he caught them both with the handle, one on the chin, the other taller man in the throat.

All five men were now either lying on the floor or on their knees. One man was down with a broken nose; another was on his back, bleeding from the cheek. A third was staggering to his feet, holding his chin, and the fourth was on his knees, his hands on his throat, gagging. Parmalee discarded the axe handle, turned and kicked the two men who were prone, just for good measure. He turned to the man who was getting to his feet, grabbed him by the hair and smashed him in the face twice with his right. He released the man, who immediately joined the other two on the floor. The fourth man was still gagging and was no danger.

That left the man who had started the whole thing. He was slumped against the bar, his eyes wide as he watched Parmalee easily dispatch the others.

"What's your name?" Parmalee asked him.

"Wha-what?"

"Your name?"

"Jenkins." Jenkins had a lump on his jaw where Parmalee had hit him.

"Straighten up, Jenkins."

Jenkins did so, using the bar to stand himself up straight.

"Open your mouth."

"What?"

Parmalee took out his gun and pointed it at Jenkins. "Open your mouth," he repeated.

Jenkins opened his mouth, and Parmalee very gently inserted the barrel of his gun, pushing until the man started to gag. Then he cocked the hammer, and Jenkins got very still. The room was quiet except for the sound of the gagging man on the floor. Parmalee guessed that some permanent damage must have been done to the man's throat.

"Take a message to your boss," Parmalee said. "Up to now I wasn't working for Ted Shea, but as of now I am. Tell him if he sends any more men to get in my way, I'll kill them. Tell him that I promise him that Ted Shea's cows are going to market, no matter who I have to go through. Do you understand all of this?"

Jenkins, his eyes wide and watery, nodded jerkily. Slowly, Parmalee removed his gun from the man's mouth.

"Get your friend here to a doctor before he chokes to death."

"Yeah, yeah. . . ." Jenkins said. He moved toward the other men, shaking the ones who were on the floor. Parmalee helped him revive them by dumping the remainder of his beer on their faces. They came awake, sputtering.

"Come on, damn it," Jenkins said. He took

hold of the choking man and pushed him toward the door. Over his shoulder he was shouting, "Let's go. . . ."

The other three, suffering from their own injuries, staggered after him.

Parmalee turned to the bartender and said, "You got your axe handle back?"

The man nodded, staring at Parmalee in awe. He had seen a lot of bar fights over the years, but never before had he seen one man take out five so quickly.

"Draw me another beer, then."

CHAPTER NINE

"On the house."

Parmalee turned and saw Nick Abel approaching him.

"If you'll accept it," Abel added.

"I almost always accept a free drink," Parmalee said, "especially after I've worked up a thirst."

"Is that what you call what you just did?" Abel asked. "Working up a thirst?"

Parmalee grabbed the beer and took a big swallow. "That was a lesson."

"What kind of lesson?"

"Five-to-one odds should always be unbeatable."

"It wasn't."

"They played it wrong," Parmalee said. "There were five of them; they should have all come at me at once. I couldn't have stopped them then, even with the axe handle."

"What about your gun?"

Parmalee smiled. "If they had all come at me at once, I would have used it."

"Against unarmed men?"

"Against five unarmed men, yes," Parmalee said. "I won't take a beating, not if I don't have to. No jury would have convicted me for using a gun against five men."

"What about a judge?"

"I try never to get into a situation where my life is in the hands of others—especially not judges."

"Well, it's out of your hands now."

"Oh? Whose hands is it in?"

"Max Venable's—that is, if you meant what you said to his man."

"I meant it."

"Why?"

"Let's just say he rubbed me the wrong way."

"Do you know who you're tangling with?"

"Sure," Parmalee said, "a man who thinks of money as a weapon."

"Isn't it?"

"Not *mano a mano*," Parmalee said. "Not against a gun."

"It can buy guns, though."

"You can buy all the guns you want, Abel," Parmalee said. "Then you've got to put them into the hands of men who are not only able to use them, but willing."

"You think you can beat Max Venable, then?"

"That's not the job I'm taking," Parmalee said. "I'm hiring on to deliver a herd of cows to market."

"Is that what you think?"

"That's it."

"You're going to have to get by Max Venable and a lot of his men to do it."

"That's just something I have to do along the way," Parmalee said, "like rounding up strays and shooting rattlesnakes."

Nick Abel looked into Parmalee's eyes and suddenly felt a chill. This man did not fear Max Venable in the slightest, and in Nick Abel's eyes, that made him quite unique.

"I envy you," Abel said.

"Why?"

"You don't have any emotions."

"Sure I do."

"Not that you let show."

"Ah," Parmalee said, smiling, "there's the secret."

"I almost wish I could go along and see it."

"Come along, then," Parmalee invited. "I'm sure Shea could use another man."

Abel laughed. "I said 'almost.' Listen, you broke even less this time than last time. You've got another drink coming."

"I'll take it."

"And a girl, if you want."

Parmalee looked over at the redhead with the freckles between her breasts and said, "Tonight I might take you up on that."

Abel followed his gaze and said, "Good choice. I'll have her in your room by—"

"Just tell her to be ready to leave when I do," Parmalee interrupted.

"All right. Oh, by the way, her name's Julie."

"Names don't matter."

Abel was going to reply, but Parmalee turned

his back to the man and concentrated on his beer. Abel turned and walked over to the redhead. She listened to what he had to say, looked over at Parmalee, and then nodded.

Four men dragged themselves back to the Venable ranch, all nursing wounds of various degrees. The fifth man, Keifer, was still at the doctor's. The medical man didn't quite know the full extent of the throat injury, but it was very possible that the man would never speak again.

As the four men dismounted, Rex Cameron approached them. He stopped short when he saw the blood and the bandages.

"Jesus H. Christ," he said. "What the hell happened?"

"Boss," one of them said, "if you want this fella Parmalee, you're gonna have to send a lot more than five men." The speaker was the man to whom Parmalee had given the message.

"Jesus," Cameron said, "one man did this to you?"

"He gave me a message for the old man," Jenkins said. "You want me to tell you, so you can tell him?"

"Hell, no," Cameron said, "you can tell him yourself. The rest of you better lie down before you fall down."

"Boss—" Jenkins began.

"Let's go, Jenkins," Cameron said. "I'll go with you, but you're gonna deliver the message yourself."

* * *

"And I thought whores were cold," the redhead, Julie, said later.

They were in Parmalee's bed and had just finished having sex. Parmalee was sitting on the edge of the bed, lighting a cigarette he had just rolled.

"If you're trying to insult me, forget it," he said, shaking the match out. "You can leave now."

This was the coldest man she had ever been with, but Julie didn't want to leave. She had been to bed with a lot of men, but even emotionless, Parmalee had brought her to heights she had only experienced once or twice before.

"Parmalee," she said, "let me spend the night."

"No."

"Please—"

"No!" he snapped.

"Why not?"

He paused before answering, then said, "I can't sleep with anyone else in the bed."

She stood up naked and posed a moment, but he didn't look at her. She shrugged and got dressed.

"There's some money on the dresser," he said.

"No money," she said. "Nick said this was part of my job."

"Then take the money and don't tell Nick."

She thought that over a moment, then said, "All right."

She paused by the door to take the money from the dresser top.

"Sure you won't change your mind—"

"Good-bye," he said. Not "Good night," but "Good-bye." That was plain enough.

She left.

* * *

"The gall of the man!" Max Venable exploded.

"You better get out of here," Cameron said to Jenkins, who wasted no time in doing so.

"Who the *hell* does he think he is?"

Cameron stood silently while the older man ranted and raved. When he had finally talked— or shouted—himself out, he sank back in his chair and frowned.

"Mr. Venable—"

"We're going to need help on this, aren't we, Cameron?" he asked finally.

"I guess so, sir. I mean, even if we send ten men after him, we're most likely gonna lose some."

"To deal with a man like this," Venable said, "we're going to need another man like this."

"Or men."

"Yes," Venable said, nodding, "or men." He looked at his foreman and asked, "Do you know any such men, Rex?"

"I do, sir."

"Then take care of it, Rex," Venable said, "take care of it."

"I will, sir."

After the girl left, Parmalee stood up and walked to the window, which overlooked the main street. He was naked and still smoking the cigarette.

No emotions, Nick Abel had said. That was a laugh. If he had no emotions, he wouldn't have made that ridiculous statement to one of Max Venable's men. He could just as easily have told the man to tell Venable that he *didn't* work for Shea, and had no intention of working for him.

Instead, he had gone and painted a bull's-eye on his back, and for what? How much could Shea pay him, anyway? Certainly not enough to risk his life for.

He opened the window, letting in a stream of cold air, and dropped the cigarette butt outside. He left the window open for a moment, then closed it. He was stuck with the job now. In the morning he'd ride out and tell Ted Shea that he had himself a hand.

CHAPTER TEN

At breakfast the next morning Ted Shea heard a horse approaching.

"Now, who could that be this early?"

"Maybe somebody who forgot to hit you yesterday," Laura said.

Her remark reminded him of how little sympathy he'd gotten the day before when he returned home. Granted, she had cleaned his injuries, but she had been very unsympathetic about how he had gotten them.

"You think your father would send someone here?"

"I gave up a long time ago trying to predict what Max will do or not do."

It was Joey who rushed to the window and looked outside.

"Pa, it's Parmalee!" she announced excitedly.

"Who?" Laura asked.

"Parmalee," Ted Shea said, rising from his chair. "The man I tried to hire yesterday."

"Do you think he's come to make sure you know he refused?" she asked. "Maybe he wants to kick you a couple of times for good measure."

Ted ignored his wife, walked to the door and opened it. Joey pushed behind him.

"Stay inside, Joey."

"But Pa—"

"Stay inside!"

She made a face, but as the door closed, she hurried to the window again. After a moment, she had to move aside to make room for her mother.

Outside, Ted Shea stepped down off his porch to wait for Parmalee to reach the house.

Parmalee dismounted and walked up to the other man. "Got any coffee for a new hand?"

Ted tried not to show his pleasure at Parmalee's words. "Got a whole breakfast, if you want it," he said. "What changed your mind?"

"I'll tell you over breakfast."

"Come on in."

At the table, Parmalee told Ted Shea what had happened the night before, in the saloon. Joey listened in rapt attention. Laura Shea fussed over Parmalee and brushed against his shoulder as she served him his food. Parmalee wondered idly why her husband couldn't see what she was doing.

"Let me get this straight," Ted said after Parmalee had finished. "You're comin' to work for me because Max already thinks you work for me?"

"Not exactly," Parmalee said. "I'm coming to

work for you because I don't like having five men sent after me for something I didn't do. I also don't like the idea that some rich man thinks he can scare me away from a job."

"Ego," Laura Shea said.

"What?"

"Your ego is making you take the job."

Parmalee looked at her in genuine puzzlement. "I don't have an ego."

"Oh, come on," she said. "Listen to the way you told us the story about beating up five men. I'll bet you exaggerated . . . just a little?"

"I never exaggerate," he said. "I told you exactly what happened."

"It's true, Ma," Joey said. "You shoulda seen him the other night."

"Never mind, Laura," Ted said. "It doesn't matter why Parmalee is comin' to work for us, just that he is." He looked at Parmalee. "Have you ever worked with cows before?"

"Yes," Parmalee said, "but not for a while."

"Cows?" Laura said. "We're not hiring him to work cows. We want his gun."

Ted started to speak, but Parmalee beat him to it.

"It's a package deal, Mrs. Shea. I work for you, and I wear a gun. If I have to use it, I will."

"Oh, you'll have to use it, all right," she assured him. "My father knows that if we don't sell these cows, we're through."

"What does he hope to gain?"

"Gain? He wants to see Ted a broken man, and he wants me and Joey to come live with him."

"I ain't livin' with Grandpa."

"You'll live where I tell you, young lady."

"What does that mean?" Ted Shea asked.

"That means that if we *don't* sell those cows, Ted, we're going to lose this place. If *that* happens, my dear husband, I won't have any choice but to take Joey and go to live with Max."

"Max?" Parmalee said.

She looked at him and said, "Max."

"Let's not discuss that now," Ted said. "Parmalee, when you finish your breakfast, I'll take you out and show you the herd. Do you have any belongings at the hotel?"

"I checked out," he said. "Everything is on my horse."

"There's a small bunkhouse out back," Ted said. "It's barely standing, but we'll be leaving at the end of the week. It should last."

"That's fine," Parmalee said. "Let's go look at that herd." He stood up, picked his hat up and put it on. Laura Shea was looking at him with her arms crossed, but he ignored her.

"You're welcome," she said as he went out the door with her husband.

"He's not very polite," Joey said.

"Clean the table, Joey."

While she did as she was told, her mother stood there with her arms crossed, staring at the door her husband and Parmalee had just gone out. Maybe Parmalee wasn't polite, but he had other . . . attributes that appealed to Laura even more.

Jesus, she thought, her hands flying to her hair, *I must look a mess*.

* * *

"I want to apologize for my wife," Ted Shea said as they rode to the herd.

"For what?"

"She was rude."

"If I remember right, you said she was going to do the cooking."

"That's right."

"Well," Parmalee said, "she cooks just fine. There's no need to apologize."

CHAPTER ELEVEN

"We're being watched."

"Where?" Ted Shea asked, looking around.

"Just keep looking at your cows, Shea," Parmalee said. "There are two men on a hill behind us."

"Max Venable's men?"

"No way I can know that for sure, but it makes sense."

"They're makin' sure that you really are working for me."

"No," Parmalee said, "I made sure they knew that last night."

"Then why?"

"Just so they'll know what we're doing."

"We're not doin' anything," Ted Shea said.

"Why are we leaving at the end of the week?"

"I still have to go to the bank and get a loan to buy supplies."

Parmalee turned his head and looked at Ted Shea. "You don't have money for supplies?"

"Don't worry," Ted said, "your money will come out of the loan."

"Is the bank owned by Max Venable?"

"No."

"But he's a major depositor."

"Of course."

"And you think you're going to get a loan?" Parmalee thought this might be his shortest job on record.

"Oh, I'll get the loan. Max will see to that."

"I don't understand."

"I'm putting my place up as collateral," Ted explained. "If I don't deliver my herd, I lose my place."

"That's what your wife meant."

"Right."

"And Venable will make sure you get the loan, and then will try to make sure you don't deliver."

"Right again. Once I deliver, I'll be able to pay the bank back, pay you, and still have enough left to keep going."

"For how long, Shea?"

"Jesus, how do I know?" Ted said. "A month? A year? Who knows?"

"Hell of a way to live."

"What about the way you live?" Ted Shea's tone was a bit testy, a side of the man Parmalee had not yet seen. Maybe it was a side he should have shown his wife more often.

Parmalee looked at him and then said, "You've got a point."

Somewhat mollified, Ted asked, "What do
do about them?"

"Nothing," Parmalee said. "Let them wa
They're not doing any harm."

"And what do we do if they decide to *do* s
harm?"

"We harm them before they harm us,"
malee replied. "Can you use that gun?"

"When I have to."

"Can you hit what you shoot at?"

"Actually," Ted confessed, "I'm better
rifle."

"How much better?"

"With a rifle I *can* hit what I aim at."

"Then forget about the handgun,"
said. "If trouble starts, use the rifle. What about
Mrs. Shea?"

"Laura? What about her?"

"Can she shoot?"

"Better than I can," Ted admitted, "with a rifle
or a handgun. Her father wanted a boy, so he
made sure she knew how to ride and shoot."

"I thought Joey said she was no good when it
came to work."

"It's not that she can't work," Ted Shea said.
Left unspoken was the fact that she *wouldn't*.
"She used to help me a lot, in the begin-
ning. . . ."

"You don't have to explain anything to me,"
Parmalee said. He didn't want to hear about Ted
Shea's marital problems—and having seen Laura
Shea, he was sure that there were plenty. "All I
need to know is who I can count on."

"Well, she'll cook, and when it comes right down to it," Ted said, "she'll shoot."

"That's good enough for me."

"Joey can ride real good, too," Ted said. "She'll be able to help with the herd."

"Wait a minute," Parmalee said. "Joey's coming with us?"

"She has to," Ted said. "I've got no place to leave her, Parmalee."

"Can't you leave her with a neighbor?"

"To tell you the truth, Parmalee," Ted Shea admitted, "I don't dare leave her behind. I might never get her back."

"Her grandfather would kidnap her?"

"He's had plenty of chances," Ted said. "I mean, she sneaks into town so often, but if I left her behind . . . I just can't take the chance."

"I didn't hire on as a baby-sitter."

"Don't worry about it," Ted said, "Joey'll earn her keep."

"It's your herd."

"Yep," Ted said, "and I want to keep it that way. I appreciate you comin' around, Parmalee."

"You better thank your father-in-law," Parmalee said. "If it wasn't for him sending those five men after me, I wouldn't be here."

"I think I'll just hold on to my thank-yous, if you don't mind."

They rode around the herd in silence for a little while, Parmalee trying to figure out how many head Ted Shea had.

"I figure about two hundred head," Parmalee guessed.

Ted Shea gave Parmalee an appraising look and

said, "Two hundred and twelve. We can handle them. I seen seven men drive a thousand head once."

"Once?"

"We can handle them," Ted said again.

"Yeah," Parmalee said, "I expect we can. How far we driving them?"

"I figure about nine hundred miles," Ted said. "If we can make twelve miles a day, we should be there in two and a half months."

"Two and a half . . . months?"

"Yeah," Ted said. "Uh, how long did you think it would take?"

"I didn't think," Parmalee said—that was his problem. He didn't think before opening his mouth, and now he had committed himself to a two-and-a-half-month trail drive.

Well, when he really thought about it, what else did he have planned for the next two and a half months?

CHAPTER TWELVE

The remainder of the week went uneventfully. Ted Shea and Parmalee took turns keeping watch on the herd, and even Joey took a turn or two. Parmalee found out that the little girl really could handle a horse, and grudgingly admitted to himself that maybe she wouldn't be such a liability after all.

The morning of the day before they were to leave, Ted Shea announced at breakfast, "I've got to go in and see the bank president today."

"He didn't approve the loan yet?" Laura asked.

"No," Ted said, "but he will. Max must have told him to make us sweat."

"Well, we're doing that, all right," she said. She looked at Parmalee, but spoke to her husband. "Is Parmalee going in with you?"

"No," Ted said, "he'll stay here and keep an eye on the herd. I'm taking Joey with me, though. She has a few little friends in town she wants to say good-bye to."

"They're not 'little' friends, Pa," Joey complained. "You know, kids really don't like bein' called little all the time."

"What would kids rather be called?" Parmalee asked.

His question drew the attention of not only Joey, but of her parents. It was the first time they had ever seen Parmalee actually direct a question toward Joey.

"Um . . . I don't know," Joey said, giving Parmalee a puzzled look, "but not little."

"I see."

Parmalee didn't speak throughout the remainder of breakfast.

After breakfast, Ted stood up and said, "We should be back within a few hours. I'm takin' the buckboard to carry the supplies."

"Are we taking the buckboard on the drive?" Parmalee asked.

"No, I have a wagon waitin' in town. Once I get the money from the bank, I'll go over to the livery and pay for it. Sam Waters, the liveryman, will bring it out tonight so we can pack it up."

"If you get the money," Laura said.

"We'll get it, Laura," Ted said, "don't worry about that. Just worry about what pots and pans and blankets and such you're goin' to pack."

"You sure you're not getting enough money to hire a cook?"

Ted Shea forced a laugh and said, "Why would we want to eat someone else's cookin' . . . right Joey?"

"Right."

Neither one of them spoke with any real assurance in their tone.

"I better get out to the herd," Parmalee said as Ted and Joey went out the door.

"Would you help me clear the table, Parmalee?"

"No, ma'am," he said, taking his hat off a peg on the wall and setting it on his head.

"What?" She placed her hands on her hips and glared at him.

"That's not part of my job, ma'am."

"Your job is to do whatever I tell you to do!"

"You're wrong again, ma'am," he said. "I work for your husband, and my job is to keep those cows safe and make sure they get delivered . . . and that's all. Anything else you want," he added pointedly, "you'll have to get from someone else."

They both knew what he was talking about, and the first time she opened her mouth to answer, she was speechless. When she finally spoke, she said, "Go on, get out of here!"

"My pleasure, ma'am."

As he went out the door, he heard her shout, "And stop calling me 'ma'am.'"

Parmalee closed the door and walked to the rundown barn to saddle his horse. Laura Shea was a handsome woman. She'd probably be a downright beautiful one if she had lived a softer life, but as it was, she was real attractive. Parmalee was becoming increasingly aware of the way she looked at him and touched him here and there with a firm hip or a hand. The last thing he needed was to get involved with his employer's wife. *Employer*. That was a laugh. For the amount of money he was being paid for this job, there *should* be some fringe benefits. He wondered if Ted Shea was really unaware of what his wife was doing, or if he was just turning a blind eye to it. Since he had to spend the next two and a half months with the man, he hoped it was the former. That would just make him a fool. The latter would make him something worse.

Parmalee saddled up and rode out to the herd. He would stay there until Ted Shea returned from town, both to keep an eye on the herd, and to keep away from Laura Shea. If she made a concerted effort to bed him in her husband's absence, he didn't know if he had the . . . moral fiber to fend her off. No, that was wrong. He *knew* he didn't have the moral fiber. The morality of bedding a married woman had never stopped him before. It was just a bad idea, in this instance, plain and simple.

There was still someone on watch, keeping an eye on him and the herd. He didn't even have to see them to know that they were there, watching him. Old Man Venable—he had learned that everyone called him that, except for his daughter, who called him Max, and Ted, who sometimes called him by his first name—wanted to keep well apprised of the goings-on at his son-in-law's place. Parmalee wondered what kind of obstacles the old man had in store for them. Bushwackers, jayhawkers, stampedes? What else? They'd have enough problems getting the majority of the herd to the railhead without whatever the old man was going to throw at them. Put it all together, and maybe this wasn't going to be a two-and-a-half-month job, after all.

* * *

"Go into town," Max Venable told Rex Cameron, "and tell that fool bank president to give my son-in-law his loan . . . today . . . in cash."

"Yes, sir."

"I don't know what the hell he's been waiting for, the fool," Venable said, shaking his head.

"I think he felt he was doing what you wanted him to do."

"Did I *tell* him to make my son-in-law sweat out the loan? No, I told him to give him the loan so that he could get his herd moving. We can't do anything until the herd is moving. You're going to handle this yourself, aren't you, Rex?"

"Yes, sir," Cameron said. "I really don't like bein' away from the ranch so long—"

"If you do what you're supposed to do," Venable said, cutting him off, "you won't be gone so long."

"Yes, sir."

"What about those men we spoke about?"

"They should be arriving tomorrow," Cameron said. "I sent telegrams earlier this week, and got quick replies."

"How many men?"

"Three."

"I hope that will be enough."

"Add in some of our own men and it should be," Cameron said.

"What are we payin' them?"

"A lot."

Venable moved a hand and said, "In the end it will be worth it."

Cameron hoped so. He knew that if things

didn't go according to plan, he was going to get the blame.

"All right, get moving," the old man said. "Shea is bound to be there when the bank opens. I want you there *before* it opens."

"Don't worry, sir," Cameron said, "I'll handle it."

"I know you will, Rex," Venable said. "I have confidence in you."

As Cameron left Venable's office, the old man thought, *I have to have confidence in someone.* He didn't have a son, and he barely had a daughter and a granddaughter. Rex Cameron was the closest thing to a son he had.

Still, that didn't mean he wouldn't deal harshly with Cameron if the foreman failed him. This was, after all, business.

Rex Cameron just barely made it to the bank before opening time. When one of the clerks recognized him, he opened the door to let him in.

"Where is Mr. Gentile?"

"He's in his office," the clerk said. His name was Wallace Tuttle, which was a perfect name for a bank clerk. He was a slender youth in his early twenties who was intimidated by Cameron, not only because of his superior size, but because of who the foreman worked for. "Uh—w-we're going to open the bank soon."

"I know." Cameron brushed past the clerk. "I have to talk to him first."

"Of course," the clerk said, but Cameron didn't hear him.

Young Tuttle watched as Cameron entered the

president's office without knocking. Nervously, the young man looked at the clock and saw that it was five minutes until banking hours. He wondered if it would be all right if he opened while Cameron was still in with the bank president.

CHAPTER THIRTEEN

Parmalee had thought that by staying out by the herd he'd be safe from Laura Shea, but that didn't turn out to be the case. After a couple of hours, he heard a horse and turned, prepared to face some of Old Man Venable's men. Instead, he saw Laura riding toward him. He turned his horse to face her and waited.

Her face was expressionless as she rode up to him.

"I made some chicken for lunch."

"Thanks."

"I thought I'd come out and have some with you," she said. "Over there, by that tree."

She turned her horse and rode over to the tree she'd indicated. He hesitated, then followed. The sun was riding high in the sky, and the tree offered them some shade. By the time he reached her, she had dismounted and spread a blanket. It occurred to him that this would be his very first goddamned picnic.

When he had dismounted and walked up to the blanket, she handed him a chicken leg. He took it with a nod and bit into it.

"I want to explain something to you," she said.

"You don't have to explain anything to me."

"Yes, I do," she said. "I haven't been very happy for quite a few years now."

He never would have guessed. He bit into the chicken again and listened.

"My husband turned out to be . . . a different man than I had thought when we first got married. He's not as . . . strong as I thought he would be."

"He seems pretty strong to me."

"You're talking about stubbornness," she said, "not strength."

"You're talking about something else, too."

"I'm talking about a lot of things," she said. "For one thing, we haven't had—haven't made love—for quite some time."

He didn't reply.

"I like making love, Parmalee," she said. "I like it a lot."

He hunkered down to deposit the chicken bone on a plate and pick up another one. She really was quite a good cook. At least he wouldn't go hungry on this drive.

"Do you find me attractive?" she asked.

"That's a stupid question," he said. "You're an attractive woman, and you know it."

"Would you like to . . . make love to me?"

"Under other circumstances."

"What other circumstances? If I wasn't married, you mean?"

"I've been with married women before, Mrs. Shea," he said, "but not when I was working for their husbands."

"I see," she said. "So, after the drive is over, and you're not working for Ted, there would be a chance?"

He hesitated a moment, then nodded and said, "Yeah, then there would be a chance."

"But not before then?"

"No," he said, "not before then."

"I see." She stood up and wiped her hands on her pants. "When you come back in, you can bring the blanket and basket with you."

"I thought you were going to have some chicken?"

She shook her head and said, "I've lost my appetite—for food, that is."

Without another word, she mounted up and rode off back toward the house. He picked up a third chicken leg and looked at the herd.

Ted Shea came out of the bank and looked down at Joey, who had been sitting on the boardwalk, waiting.

"Did you get it?" she asked.

"I got it, honey," he said. "Let's go shopping."

"Can I get some candy?"

"Sure, honey," he said, putting his hand on her shoulder, "you can get some candy."

After talking to the bank manager, Rex Cameron went to the telegraph office to check for messages, just in case one of the men he hired was going to be late. There was nothing for him, so he rode back to the ranch. As he rode past the general store, he saw Ted Shea and his daughter going inside. It occurred to him that meant that Parmalee was alone at the ranch with Laura.

When he got back to the Venable ranch, he went to the old man's office to tell him that his son-in-law had the money he needed.

"Good," Venable said, "now I've got another job for you."

"What's that?"

"Go over to my son-in-law's place and invite Mr. Parmalee over here for a talk."

"A talk? About what?"

"It occurs to me that men like Parmalee work for money," Venable explained. "I can certainly pay him more than my son-in-law can."

Cameron noted that Venable never referred to Ted Shea by name. He always called him his son-in-law. Also, he never referred to the ranch as "my daughter's place," but always "my son-in-law's."

"And if he doesn't want to come?"

"What are you going to do?" Venable asked. "Force him? If he doesn't want to come, he won't come. Make sure he knows that it will be in his best interest, though."

"I'll tell him."

As Cameron started to leave, Venable said, "When's the last time you saw Laura, Rex?"

Cameron turned and said, "I saw her in town just last week."

"When did you speak to her last?"

"Oh," Cameron said, "not for . . . years?"

"That's what I thought."

Cameron waited, and when Venable said nothing else, he left. He was actually glad that he had a reason to ride over to Shea's place. He'd been trying to figure out a reason to go ever since he'd realized that Laura was there alone with Parmalee.

Now he had one.

It was after Cameron had left to go to town that Venable had realized a man like Parmalee could most likely be bought. He wondered why he hadn't thought of it before.

Maybe, he thought with some surprise, he was getting old.

On the way to see Parmalee, Cameron stopped to talk to Ben Snow, who was watching the Shea place at the moment.

"Anything happenin'?"

"Nothin' much," Snow reported. "The old man's daughter was out there about half an hour ago."

"Doin' what?"

"Well," Snow said, "it looked like they was gonna have a picnic, but then she left and Parmalee ate alone."

Cameron looked down toward the herd and saw Parmalee sitting on his horse, alone.

"Hey, boss . . . ?"

"Yeah?"

"Parmalee . . . is he as good as they say he is?"

"You'll have to ask Harry Pringle that," Cameron said, "if you can find him."

Cameron nudged his horse's ribs and started down the hill toward the herd.

CHAPTER FOURTEEN

This time when Parmalee heard a horse approaching, he was fairly sure that it wasn't Laura Shea. He turned and saw a lone man. Up on the hill there was still a man watching, so this was somebody new.

The man stopped about ten feet away from him, and the two appraised each other. Parmalee saw a man well over six feet, broad shoulders, in his thirties. He wore a gun on his hip, but from the look of it, it did not get much use, or care. Obviously, the gun was not used by the man in his day-to-day job.

"Can I help you?"

"My name's Rex Cameron." The man waited, as if Parmalee should recognize the name. When Parmalee did not make a comment, he went on. "I'm the foreman at the Venable place."

"Congratulations," Parmalee said. "Must be a fine-paying job."

"I have a message for you from Mr. Venable."

"The old man himself," Parmalee said. "I'm impressed. What's the message?"

"Mr. Venable would like you to come by his place and talk to him."

"About what?"

"He didn't tell me that," Cameron said. "All he said was that it would be to your advantage."

"Is that right?"

"Yeah."

Parmalee studied the man for a few moments, and Cameron stoically withstood the appraisal.

"All right," Parmalee finally said. "Tell Old Man Venable I'll be by later today for that little talk."

"I'll tell *Mister* Venable that you accept his invitation."

As Cameron began to turn his horse, Parmalee said, "Hey."

Cameron looked back over his shoulder.

"How long have you worked for the old man?"

"I've worked for Mister Venable for about fifteen years."

"Then you knew Mrs. Shea before she got married?"

"That's right. What about it?"

"Nothing," Parmalee said. "I was just asking."

Cameron stared at him for a moment, then nodded and turned away. Parmalee noticed that as the foreman rode off he veered away from the hill.

He was riding toward the house.

Cameron didn't really know that he was going to go and talk to Laura until he left Parmalee. His intention had been to ride back up the hill, but as he left Parmalee, he found himself riding toward the house.

As he approached the house, the door opened and Laura stepped out. She had probably heard the horse. When she saw who it was, she looked surprised . . . and maybe a little disappointed, as well.

"Laura," Cameron said.

"What the hell are you doing here, Rex?"

He didn't answer right away, but dismounted.

"Don't bother," she said, but he didn't stop. "You can't come in."

"That's all right," he said, wrapping the horse's reins around a nearby post. "We can talk out here."

"About what?"

"About something we should have talked about a long time ago."

"And what's that?" she asked, folding her arms across her chest.

"Us."

She stared at him for several moments, and then started laughing.

"What's so funny?" he asked, frowning.

"There is no us, Rex," she said. "There never was, and there never could be."

"And why not?"

"Because you work for my father," she said. "I'd never have anything to do with a man who works for my father."

"Is that what attracted you to Shea, then? That he wouldn't work for your father?"

"Well, of course," she said. "Back then he was the only man who wasn't afraid of the old man."

"I'm not afraid of him."

She laughed again. "You were then," she said. "Remember that time in the stable? I *wanted* you to make love to me then. Remember? And you ran off because you were afraid of him."

"I—I—"

"Never mind, Rex," she said. "What are you doing around here, anyway? You didn't ride over here to talk to me."

"I—had a message to Parmalee from your father."

"Really?" she said with interest. "And what was the message?"

"Your father wants to talk to him," Cameron said. "He's gonna buy him off."

"Not Parmalee," she said with assurance.

"And why not?"

"He can't be bought."

Now Cameron laughed. "He *works* for money."

"And he's working for us," she said. "Max won't be able to buy him off."

"We'll see."

"Yes, we will," she said.

It was then that Cameron realized that Laura was interested in Parmalee. He recalled what the man on the hill had said about a picnic.

"How sure are you that he won't be bought?"

"Dead sure."

"Sure enough to bet?"

"Bet what?"

Cameron paused and looked her up and down.

"Why, Rex," she said, "I do believe you've developed some backbone over the years."

"If he's bought," Cameron said, "your trail drive will be dead, and you'll lose this place."

"So?"

"For my end of the bet I want you," Cameron said.

"Me?"

"You know what I mean."

"Yes," she said, "I do. All right, Rex. If you win the bet, you can have me . . . but it will have to be in my father's stable, from where you fled all those years ago."

Cameron hesitated.

"What's wrong?" she asked. "I thought you weren't afraid of him."

"I'm not," Cameron said sharply. "All right."

"And for my end of the bet . . ." she said thoughtfully.

"What?"

"I can't think of anything I could want from *you* right now, but I will," she said. "When the time comes, I'll think of something."

Cameron stood there for a few moments more before he realized that she had nothing more to say to him.

"All right," he said, and mounted his horse. "You'll see I've changed, Laura. You'll find out."

As Cameron rode away, Laura found herself wondering if he had changed after all.

"Nah," she said, after a moment, "not likely."

Parmalee hesitated a moment after Cameron left, and then decided the herd could go unguarded for a few moments. He looked up at the man on the hill and doubted that he would be rustling the whole herd by himself. Besides, he wanted to see Cameron and Laura Shea together, just to satisfy his curiosity.

And so he watched. . . .

After Cameron left, Laura Shea stayed on the porch for a few moments. As she started to turn to go back in, she saw Parmalee watching her. Had he been watching the whole time? Probably. She smiled, stifled an urge to wave to him, and went back inside.

CHAPTER FIFTEEN

When Ted and Joey Shea returned from town with all the supplies they needed for the drive, neither Parmalee nor Laura mentioned Rex Cameron's visit, or Max Venable's invitation for Parmalee to visit him.

After Parmalee had helped Ted unload the buckboard and load up the chuck wagon Shea had bought in town, he told Ted that he had to leave for a while.

"To do what?"

"Tie up some loose ends," Parmalee said. "I'll be back later."

"In time for dinner?"

"I don't know," Parmalee said. "Go ahead and eat without me."

Ted frowned. "Laura might not want to feed you when you get back."

"I'm not worried," Parmalee said.

"All right," Ted said, "but be back early. We're

leaving in the morning, and there's still a lot of work to be done to get ready for the trip."

"I'll be back before dark."

"Good."

Again, Parmalee found himself wondering about Ted Shea. He was entirely too easygoing for Parmalee's taste. He liked the men he worked for to be stronger in their dealings with both their families—in this case, Laura Shea—and their employees—namely Parmalee. Ted should have asked more questions about where Parmalee was going and what he would be doing.

Parmalee saddled up and headed for Max Venable's ranch. As he rode off, he thought he saw someone watching him from the window. He couldn't be sure, but he thought it was Laura Shea.

What, he wondered, would she tell her husband in his absence?

When Parmalee came within sight of the Venable ranch, he was impressed. It was a huge, sprawling place, at the center of which stood a very big, two-story house. Parmalee knew that rich men like Venable usually made their money off the sweat of others. He may have been impressed with the size of the ranch, but he wouldn't be impressed with the man who had built it.

As he rode up to the front of the house, he became the center of attention as men stopped what they were doing to study him. They were wondering who he was, although some of them may have already known. Those who didn't, though, were wondering if they would be working side-by-side with him soon as a new hand, or if he was there to cause trouble.

One man moved away from the others on an intercept course with him, and they met at the foot of the steps leading up to the porch.

"Parmalee," Cameron said. "You're just in time."

"For what?" Parmalee asked, dismounting.

"Dinner, if you like. Mr. Venable asked me to invite you to dine with him if you arrived early enough."

Parmalee remembered what Ted had told him about Laura not feeding him if he missed dinner.

"I accept his invitation, both to talk and to eat."

"Give your horse over to Len, there, and follow me inside."

A man came and took Parmalee's horse from him, and he followed Cameron up the steps.

Inside, Cameron showed Parmalee where he could wash his hands and then led him to the dining room. At the head of a table that could have held the twelve apostles and more sat an old man. As Parmalee entered, the man pressed his palms to the table and pushed himself to a standing position.

"Are you Parmalee?"

"Yes."

"Max Venable."

Venable was . . . old. He was tall, thin, pale, bent, white-haired, watery-eyed . . . he was old, but there was still strength in him. It showed in the way his gaze held Parmalee's and refused to move away.

"Come," Venable said, beckoning with his arm, "we'll eat, and then we'll talk."

"If you don't mind," Parmalee said. "I'd rather eat *and* talk. I don't have much time."

Venable shrugged and sat down. There was another place already set at the table to Venable's right, so Parmalee took it.

"Rex, have the cook serve, will you?"

"Would you like me to join you?"

Venable looked his foreman right in the eye and said, "No."

Cameron went into the kitchen, and Parmalee did not see him again until he left the house. Moments later a woman came out carrying a tray and set plates of food in front of them. From the looks of it, it was stew, and from the smell, it was going to be very good. Parmalee suddenly realized that he was hungry.

"Would you like a glass of wine with dinner?" Venable asked. "My doctor has limited me to a glass after dinner, but—"

"Could we do away with the old man act?" Parmalee asked. "I'm sure if you wanted to drink a gallon of wine there is no one who could stop you."

Venable stared at Parmalee for what seemed like a long period of time and then said, "I can't help lookin' old, but I will try not to sound it anymore."

"This is very good stew," Parmalee said.

"To hell with the stew," Venable said, putting his fork down. "How much will it take for you to stop working for my son-in-law?"

"More than you've got."

"I doubt that."

"Don't."

Parmalee continued to eat while Venable tried to figure out a reply.

"Are you aware of how much money I'm worth?"

"A lot."

"A hell of a lot *more* than a lot."

"Mr. Venable," Parmalee said, looking at the man now, "if I were interested in money in the first place, would I be working for what your son-in-law is paying me?"

"I wondered about that myself," Venable said. "A man like yourself—"

"And what kind of man is that?"

"What?"

Parmalee put down his fork now and gave Max Venable all his attention. "I'm interested in what kind of man it is you think I am."

Venable frowned and asked, "Is this a test? You're a gunman. You sell your gun to the highest bidder."

"I'll ask you the same question," Parmalee said. "Would I be working for—"

"All right, damn it!" Venable yelled. "Why *are* you working for my son-in-law?"

"He has a name, you know."

"Just answer the question."

Parmalee leaned forward, pushing his plate out of the way of his elbows. "I'm working for *Ted Shea* because of you."

"Me?"

"You sent some of your men after me, Venable," Parmalee said. "I didn't like that."

"So they found out. You handle yourself very well, I understand. What I don't understand is why you didn't kill them."

"There was no need. The man I was a few years ago might have killed them, but. . . ."

"Ah, I see," Venable said, a crafty look coming into his eyes, "you've changed. . . ."

"Men do change."

"Not men like you."

"Again, you think you know what kind of man I am."

"I do," Venable said, and he leaned forward this time. "I know exactly who you are . . . now."

Parmalee sat back in his chair and said, "I think you're going to have to explain that remark."

CHAPTER SIXTEEN

"Let's forget this dinner," Venable said. He stood up, considerably more quickly and easily than he had when Parmalee first entered the room. "Let's go into my office and have a drink."

"Wine?"

Venable made an impatient gesture with his hand and said, "Something stronger."

Parmalee followed Venable through the house to his office.

"Have a seat," Venable said as they entered. "Scotch whiskey?"

"Fine."

Venable poured two tumblers of Scotch, handed Parmalee one and sat behind his desk with his drink. Parmalee tasted his and found it very good. He had to make sure he didn't like it too much, though. He wouldn't be getting any more after this.

"I know you, Parmalee," Venable said. "You hate people who have money. That means you hate me, even though you don't know me. You're an intelligent man. Does that make sense?"

"Not the way you say it."

"Then how would you say it?"

"I hate men with money who think that because they have it, they can do anything they want, buy anyone they want."

"And so you can't be bought."

"Not by you."

"Because you think you know me?"

"I know you at least as well as you know me."

That stopped the conversation cold, and they both sucked on their drinks until the glasses were empty.

"So?" Venable asked.

"Time for me to go." Parmalee stood up.

"You're givin' up a lot of money, Parmalee."

"I know."

"That doesn't bother you?"

"No," Parmalee said. "I've learned to get by on very little money. I can actually do it quite well."

Venable frowned. "That's something I've never learned to do, something I never had to learn to do. I was born to money, Parmalee, lots of it, but I've increased the fortune that was left to me tenfold."

"Is that supposed to impress me?"

"No. I was just commenting. . . . If you don't take my money, Parmalee, your life could be in danger."

"Is that a threat?"

"No. If you insist on going with my son-in-law, there will be a lot of danger ahead of you."

"As there is on any cattle drive."

"But there will be only two of you."

"Four."

"Four?"

"Mrs. Shea and Joey will be going along."

Venable didn't like that.

"My granddaughter—"

"So you see, Venable," Parmalee said slowly, "anything that happens to me on this drive could also happen to . . . her."

Venable stood up more quickly than Parmalee would have thought possible.

"Don't think you can hide behind my granddaughter, Parmalee," the older man said slowly. He pointed a rock-steady finger at Parmalee. "You are making a very bad enemy in me."

"That's just as well," Parmalee said, "considering the alternatives." Parmalee walked to the office door, then turned and added, "I doubt we would ever have been very trusting friends."

As Parmalee left, Max Venable couldn't help but agree with him.

Outside, Parmalee found Rex Cameron waiting for him. The foreman was holding Parmalee's horse.

"How was dinner?" Cameron asked.

"Delicious," Parmalee said, "what there was of it. It was . . . cut a bit short."

He took the reins of his horse from Cameron and turned the animal around.

"And the talk?"

Parmalee mounted up. "*That* was interesting."

Cameron hesitated, then asked, "And rewarding?"

Parmalee allowed himself a cold, humorless smile and said, "Only spiritually."

As Parmalee rode away, Cameron assumed that meant that Venable had been unable to buy Parmalee off.

He had lost his bet with Laura Shea. That made him angry—with Laura, with Parmalee, and even with Max Venable. Through his anger, he wondered what Laura would ask as payment for the bet.

CHAPTER SEVENTEEN

Camped outside of town, Felix Hankman watched Preston Walton cook their dinner over the campfire. Hankman and Walton had worked together many times before, and when paired, Walton did all the cooking. He claimed that he'd rather die from a bullet than from Hankman's cooking.

Felix Hankman—called "Hank" more often than not—was forty-five and had been making his way with a gun since he killed his first man at seventeen. He did not keep count of the number of men he had killed over the years, but having been involved in many wars—from range wars to the Civil War—he would probably have guessed the number to be in the hundreds. Hankman was tall and whipcord thin, and always had been, even though he had a huge appetite. He had thinning dark hair and a well-cared-for mustache that was his only vanity.

On the other hand, Preston Walton—called

"Walt"—knew exactly how many men he had killed between the ages of twenty-two and forty-one. Not counting the Civil War, he had killed fifty-nine men. If you had asked him how many of them had been killed face to face, the number would drop to ten. Walton was a notorious back-shooter, and proud of it. He was fond of saying that most men he had killed were faster and better with a gun than he was; but he was alive and they were dead, and that's what counted—not *where* you shot them.

Preston Walton was not an imposing-looking man. In fact, he looked rather ordinary. He was about five-eight, a good thirty pounds overweight, and he managed never to look clean. The only thing he and Hankman had in common was their thinning dark hair.

Walton dished out the beans and bacon and handed Hankman a plate.

"Who's the other man comin' in on this?" Hankman asked. It had been Preston Walton who had been contacted by Rex Cameron, and he had brought Hankman into the play, as well as the third man.

"Harry."

Hankman stared. "Harry 'the Hat' Ross?"

"Is there another Harry?"

Hankman chewed his bacon and shook his head. "I don't like working with Ross."

"Why not?"

"That big, white, wide-brimmed hat he wears all the time," Hankman said. "It makes him a target, and I don't like being around a target."

"This Venable has a lot of money, and he

wanted the best," Walton said, using his fork to point. "That's you, me, and Harry the Hat."

"How many are we goin' up against?"

"I don't know," Walton said with a shrug. "We'll find all that out when we get there. All I know is we're gettin' paid a lot."

"As long as it ain't any army," Hankman said. "I hate facin' an army with only three men. The two times we did that we almost got killed."

"Yeah, but we didn't," Walton reminded him. "We made lots of money. This time, though, we're gonna make a *really* lot of money."

Hankman looked thoughtful and said, "You know, I've spent a lot of money over the years, but I don't think I've ever had the chance to spend a *really* lot of money. How long do you think that would take, Walt?"

"The way you spend money? Not a hell of a long time, Hank."

Camped on the other side of town, Harry "the Hat" Ross ate a solitary meal of coffee and beef jerky. He could have ridden on into town, but his instructions from Preston Walton had been not to ride into town until the next morning, Friday. Since there was a lot of money involved, Ross was willing to blindly follow instructions . . . for now.

Harry Ross was thirty-five, and for ten of those years—the last ten, of course—he had been Harry the Hat, all because he found a hat he liked in a Denver haberdashery. It was a huge, wide-brimmed, white hat that he took care of like it were a baby. It had a nick or two from flying lead, but all in all it was in excellent shape for a hat he had been wearing for ten years.

The hat was set aside now, resting atop his saddlebags to keep it off the ground. He ran his hand through thick brown hair, then decided to clean his weapon for want of something better to do. He didn't take as good care of his guns as he did the hat, but he always made sure they were in proper working order when he was riding into a new job.

Harry the Hat's reputation was exactly the opposite of Preston Walton's. He had never killed a man who wasn't facing him. If asked how many men he had killed, he would probably be able to answer fairly accurately, but it would take him a few moments of heavy thinking. Harry was used to quick action, not heavy thinking.

He was coming to this job right from his last one. He never took time off between jobs if he could avoid it. He didn't like having time on his hands. He didn't know what to do with it. If he wasn't working, he was looking for work. Harry Ross was very good, and very reliable, and that's why he was able to work constantly. In fact, that's also why, after so many years of working, he was still alive.

As he lifted his rifle, his gaze fell upon his hat. He thought he noticed a smudge on the rim, so he set the rifle down and lifted the hat. He didn't get back to his weapons for some time after that.

There was a lot to be done, and all four of them—the Sheas and Parmalee—worked until almost midnight making preparations for leaving. After seeing to the herd and making sure that they had everything in the wagon they needed, Parmalee and Shea nailed all the windows closed.

"What's the point?" Laura asked as they were working. "This shack will still be here when we get back. Come on, Joey. Time for bed."

After Laura and Joey had gone to bed, Ted and Parmalee had a cigarette outside before turning in.

"Shack," Ted mumbled, almost to himself.

"What?"

"Oh, nothing . . . I just said . . . shack."

Parmalee kept looking at Ted, waiting for him to explain the remark.

"Laura, she called this house a shack. When I first built it, she called it *home*."

"That was a long time ago, wasn't it?"

"Yes," Ted said, "a long time ago."

"People change."

Ted looked at Parmalee and then asked, "Is that what you and Max talked about today?"

Parmalee may have been surprised by the question, but he did not show it.

"That and other things."

"Money?"

"Sure," Parmalee said, "we talked about money."

"How much did he offer you?"

Parmalee looked at Ted and said, "We didn't get down to a real number. He just said it was a lot of money."

"Well, with Max, a lot is a *lot*."

Parmalee didn't comment.

"I take it you didn't accept his offer?"

"No."

Ted nodded, looked like he was going to ask another question, then nodded again and dropped his cigarette on the ground. "We'll get started at first light."

"I'll be there."

Ted nodded for the third time in sixty seconds and went inside. Parmalee shook his head, dropped his cigarette to the ground, and went to bed down.

Max Venable couldn't sleep. He got out of bed and walked to the window. It was at times like this—this and waking in the middle of the night—when he missed his wife. His Flora had been a beautiful woman, and she'd lent her beauty to her daughter, Laura. When Laura had married Shea against his will, Max had thought that it would last a year, maybe two, and then she would come back. After Joey had been born—Josephine Flora Shea—he'd thought perhaps that would do it, but no, Laura stood by Shea. In a way, he admired her for the way she had stuck to her man. It was what her mother had done before her. Of course, Max and Flora had never been dirt poor; but they had had their hard times, and Flora had never flinched.

Of late, however, Max thought he saw Laura flinching. When he saw her in town, the hard set of her face told him she was not happy. He hoped that after this trail drive failed she would come back to him, with Joey, before her life with Shea robbed her of the legacy of her mother's beauty. Joey would be beautiful, too, if he could get her away from Shea in time.

Venable thought back to early that evening. . . .

* * *

After Parmalee had left, Venable had called Rex Cameron into his office.

"He wouldn't be bought?" Cameron asked.

"No."

"Maybe you didn't offer him—" Cameron started, but he stopped short. He realized Max Venable would have offered Parmalee plenty. If Parmalee hadn't taken it, he had to have a reason.

"It is his misfortune that he would not be bought," Venable said. "Are your men comin' in tomorrow?"

"Yes."

"Who are they?"

"Preston Walton, Felix Hankman—"

"I never heard of them."

"—and Harry Ross."

Venable gave his foreman a sharp look. "Harry the Hat?"

"That's him."

Now the look turned to one of satisfaction. "Well, well . . . that's more like it."

"The other two are good men," Cameron said. "Walton is the one I contacted. I told him to bring in two other men. He got Hankman and Ross."

"You've done well, Rex . . . now let's hope they can get the job done."

"They'll get it done, sir. . . ."

Venable hoped they would get it done. In fact, he would speak to them himself, and make them understand that he would even have them destroy Ted Shea in order to get his daughter back.

CHAPTER Eighteen

Parmalee came awake immediately. Instinct told him that daylight was still hours away. Someone was moving around outside the bunkhouse. His gun was very near, and he reached out now and grabbed it. He remained on the pallet, lying on his side, facing the door. If they were going to come in that way, they were in for a surprise, but he was prepared for them to try a window, try to catch him off guard.

Was Venable impatient? Did he want to take Parmalee out of the picture now instead of somewhere along the trail? And if so, who had he sent? Cameron? Another cowhand? No, with Venable's money, he could have had his pick of gunmen to send after Parmalee.

Who would it be?

Whoever it was, they would find a kill fee on Parmalee the hardest money they ever tried to earn.

Parmalee, his eyes well adjusted to the darkness inside the small bunkhouse, kept his gaze on the doorknob and noticed immediately when it first started to turn. He cocked the hammer on his gun and waited.

The door swung inward, and a small, silhouetted figure slipped into the room. He slid the hammer off cock and sat up on the pallet.

"What are you doing here?"

"I couldn't sleep," Joey said. "Can I talk to you?"

"Joey, it's late," he said, "and we have to get an early start in the—"

"Is it all children you don't like," she asked, "or just me?"

"What?"

"I know you don't like me," she said. "Is it something I done?"

"Joey . . . I don't *dis*like you."

"But you don't like me."

He put the gun down on the pallet beside him. She remained by the door. There was a storm lamp next to the pallet, and he lifted it, lit it, and adjusted the glow so that there was a soft light just barely illuminating the room.

"Who says I don't like you?"

"You never talk to me," she said. "You hardly ever look at me. What am I supposed to think?"

He rubbed his hand over his face and realized that he was clad only in his long underwear. Well, what did she expect him to be wearing?

"Joey . . . I haven't had much experience with kids, you know?" he said. "Maybe I just don't know how to act around them."

"You have a reputation, you know."

"I know," he said. He was starting to give up any hope of getting back to sleep.

"I've heard people say how cold you are, but I don't think you are."

"No?"

"No," she said. She found a chair and sat down in it, settling her hands into her lap. She was wearing a white flannel nightgown that had gotten dirty around the hem from her walk around the house to the bunkhouse. "I think you're afraid."

"Lots of people are afraid."

"Are you?"

"You just said I was."

"I'm a kid," she said. "That was a guess. I could be wrong."

"That's nice to hear."

"What is?"

"Someone admitting that they could be wrong."

She frowned. "I think you're tryin' to get me off the subject."

"What is the subject, Joey?" he asked. He leaned over, snagged his canteen and took a swig of water. "Just what is it we're talking about here?"

"People," she said, "and how they treat other people."

"And how is that?"

"With courtesy. We're going to be spending the next two and a half months together. Even if you don't like me, I would like to be treated with courtesy."

He frowned and asked, "How old are you?"

"I'm ten."

He shook his head slightly. That was hard to believe.

"I tell you what," he said. "If you let me go back to sleep, I will do my best to treat you as courteously as I can. Is that a deal?"

She slid off the chair and said, "It's a deal."

She started for the door, then turned. She was obviously not through with him.

"What is it?"

"Do you have a first name?"

"Yes. It's Dan."

"Can I call you Dan?"

"No," he said, "you can call me Parmalee."

"Parmalee," she said, "will you keep my daddy alive for the next two and a half months?"

"That's what I'm being paid for, Joey."

She assumed a thoughtful pose, frowning, standing hipshot to the right, and said, "My daddy can't be payin' you an awful lot."

"That's between him and me, isn't it?"

"I suppose so," she said. "Good night, Parmalee."

"Good night, Joey."

She opened the door and stepped out, closing it gently behind her. He lay back on the pallet and stared at the ceiling for a while. Finally he admitted that he just wasn't going to fall back asleep, so he got up, got dressed and went out to check on the horses.

Parmalee's horse was a big roan gelding of seven years. He'd had him since the animal was three and won him off a man in a marathon poker game. He had never bothered to name the animal.

He checked the horse and found him sound, then checked the horse that would be pulling the wagon. He was running his hands up and down Ted Shea's horse's legs when he heard someone enter the barn from behind him. He drew his gun and turned quickly, then put it up when he saw Laura Shea.

"You're up early," he said.

"I don't deserve to be shot for it."

He holstered his gun and went back to what he had been doing, inspecting the legs of Ted's bay.

"What did my father have to say to you?"

"He offered me a lot of money to go away."

"And you didn't take it?"

"No."

"Why not? Are you that noble?"

Still crouched down by the horse, he looked up at her. "It has nothing to do with being noble," he said. "I work for your husband. I don't switch employers in midstream."

"If you did, who could do anything about it?"

"I don't do it," he said, again.

"Is that a rule?"

He thought a moment, then said, "More like a law."

"Parmalee's law?"

"I guess so."

"And not sleeping with your employer's wife? Is that another of Parmalee's laws?"

"No," he said, "that's just good sense. You didn't come out here to offer me your lily-white body, did you?"

"No, of course not," she said. "I came to check the horses."

"Well, there's two more after this one," he said, lifting the bay's leg so that he could study the hoof. "Be my guest."

Laura hesitated, then walked over to Joey's milk-colored mare and began to run her hands up and down the animal's legs. Parmalee looked at her once, admiring the way she was packed into her jeans, then looked away.

Laura had noticed him looking at her, and smiled.

When Ted and Joey Shea entered the livery, Parmalee and Laura were hitching the team to the wagon.

"You two are up early," Ted said.

Parmalee looked at Joey, then said, "I wanted to check the stock."

"I'll make some coffee," Laura offered.

"That's all we'll have time for," Ted Shea said.

The Sheas all looked well rested to Parmalee. He doubted that he looked the same. He wondered, though, which of them would be the first to falter on this trail drive. If he had to bet money, he would have put it on Laura. This meant too much to Ted for it to be him, and Joey's youth and energy would see her through. Although this *should* have meant at least as much to Laura as it did to Ted, Parmalee doubted it.

Parmalee saddled his roan while Ted saddled his and made Joey saddle her own. It took her longer than the two men, but she finally got the job done. Her bay was young; it would be able to keep up the pace they were going to set. He hoped that the little girl's horse would be able to match her strength and her energy.

After they drank the coffee, they walked the wagon outside for Laura. They hadn't stopped to eat, but Laura had made Joey some bacon. Parmalee watched as the little girl popped a saved last piece into her father's mouth. There was no denying the bond that existed between father and daughter. Even Laura, mother and wife, seemed an outsider.

"We'll ride to the herd and get them moving," Ted said to Laura. "Make a last-minute check of your supplies because we're not going to be stopping for more for a pretty long while."

She nodded. "All right."

"When you're satisfied, you can meet us where the road to town forks."

"All right."

Ted walked to Laura and placed his hands on her shoulders. "I know it's been hard, Laura," he said, "and over the next two months or so it's going to get harder . . . but we'll make it. I promise you, we'll make it."

She gave him a wan smile, and he kissed her on the forehead, walked to his horse and mounted up.

"Let's get this drive going," he said to Parmalee and Joey.

CHAPTER NINETEEN

Ted Shea began keeping a diary the first day out. The first entry read: "Started for Ellsworth, Kansas, with four people, two hundred and twelve head, one wagon with a team of two horses, a three-horse remuda that we strung to the back of the wagon. Parmalee and I handled the cattle well on day one. We traveled about twelve miles, which was according to schedule. Joey stayed with Laura in the wagon. Tonight Parmalee and I will take turns standing watch. I won't use Joey for any hard work unless we absolutely have to."

SECOND ENTRY: "It rained, which slowed us down some. We made about eight miles and camped for the night."

THIRD DAY: "Cold, rainy, windy. Had to use Joey because the storm was scattering the herd too much. She did a wonderful job. We're not using her on watch because she's tuckered out, poor thing. Parmalee and I are tuckered out, too, but we don't have the luxury of bedding down early. Laura's been feeding us well, even though we're rationing. No second helpings. Well, not too many."

END OF THE FIRST WEEK: "In seven days I figure we've covered about seventy miles. The insistent rain has held us back, but ten miles a day is still a decent pace. Joey's worked hard the past three days. Parmalee may have a reputation with a gun, but he's as fine a cattleman as I've ever seen. If he ever decided to put his gun away, I think he could make a go of it. Hell, I'd hire him in a minute.

"No trouble from Max's men, yet. So far we've only struggled with Mother Nature. We lost twelve head in a mud slide, eight full-grown and four calves. I'm glad we don't have too many calves in the herd. I don't think they would survive the trip."

DAY TEN: "Wet, cold morning. Traveled ten miles and camped for the night."

END OF THE SECOND WEEK: "Fourteen days on the trail. We've still got two hundred head, and the rain has let up. We've covered thirty-six miles in the past three days. All told, about one hundred fifty miles. We've crossed into Wyoming. The route I've mapped out will take us through Nebraska, Colorado, and then Kansas.

"No sign of Max's men. What are they waiting for?"

DAY TWENTY: "Thought for a moment that we had been hit during the night, but twenty head seemed to have wandered off. I wanted to hunt for the beeves, but Parmalee insisted I stay with the main herd. Used Joey while Parmalee was off hunting."

DAY TWENTY-ONE: "Was worried for a while, especially Laura, who said that Parmalee had ridden off and left us alone. Joey said she didn't believe it. Joey seems to have come to trust and like Parmalee pretty well, so I believed her."

DAY TWENTY-TWO: "Parmalee returned today with fifteen head. He did a fine job to bring back that many. We're down to 195 beeves. Joey took great satisfaction in Parmalee's return. She has really taken to this man, which I find strange. Although he does speak to her more often than he did, I still see no sign of warmth in his attitude toward her. He is an odd man. Perhaps he is simply able to mask his feelings. I hope that Joey will not end up being disappointed."

DAY TWENTY-THREE: "Joey's horse stepped in a chuck hole. It wasn't *her* horse, but one of the remuda. Leg snapped in two, and Parmalee put a bullet in its brain. Joey wasn't hurt, but she cried when Parmalee shot the horse."

DAY TWENTY-FIVE: "Traveled about five miles,

and are laying over to get some rest for us as well as the horses and the cattle. Saw some antelope tracks, and Parmalee took Joey hunting. Came back with a side of venison, which Laura butchered and cooked up deliciously. In the morning, we'll be ready to roll again, rested and well fed."

END OF WEEK FOUR: "Twenty-eight days on the trail. Still have 195 head, still no sign of Max's men, or any other possible trouble. Even the elements seem to have calmed down. Laura is even starting to show some optimism that we might make it.

"Still, four weeks is not even the halfway point, is it?"

DAY THIRTY: "We'll be camping near Dennison, a town on the border between Wyoming and Nebraska. We're using a little box canyon that will make it easy for Joey and Laura to watch the herd. Parmalee and I will be going into town tomorrow for the first time since we started the drive. The venison is gone, and food stores are low. Time to go shopping."

The morning they were to go to Dennison, Joey came to Parmalee while he was saddling his horse.

"Parmalee?"

"Yeah?"

"Will you look after my pa in town?"

Parmalee looked down at her. "Your pa can look after himself, Joey."

"I know," she said, "but you could look after him, just a little extra, couldn't you?"

He opened his mouth to say something, thought better of it, and then said, "I don't see why not."

She smiled and said, "Thanks."

She started off, and he turned to finish saddling his horse. From behind him he heard her add hurriedly, "And look after yourself, too."

As they mounted up to leave, Ted said to Laura, "You keep your rifle well at hand. We'll try not to be too long in town."

"Don't worry about us," Laura said. "Just bring back some food—and don't get into any poker games."

Of course, the worry was not that they would lose their money in a poker game. The worry was that one of them alone might get robbed of the money, so that was why they were both going.

"Don't worry," Ted said to Laura, "no poker games."

From their vantage point, Hankman, Walton and Harry the Hat watched Parmalee and Ted Shea ride off toward the town of Dennison.

"What do we do now?" Hankman asked. "Go after the cattle, or the men?"

"The men," Harry said.

Walton looked at him.

"We're being paid to take Parmalee out, right?" Harry the Hat asked.

"Right," Walton said. He looked at Hankman, who shrugged. "All right, then," Walton continued. "We'll let them get to town and then make our move."

"What about the beeves?" Hankman said.

"I ain't a drover," Harry the Hat said.

"No," Walton said, "neither am I. Once Parmalee's dead, Shea won't be able to drive the herd himself. He'll lose it. That'll be good enough for Old Man Venable."

They all agreed, Hankman grudgingly. As they headed for town, Hankman wondered how they were going to take Parmalee. Walton would naturally want to shoot him in the back, but Harry the Hat liked a challenge. He'd want to face Parmalee head on.

It was going to be interesting.

CHAPTER TWENTY

Dennison was modest as towns went, but that didn't matter to Ted Shea and Parmalee. All they were after was a general store, and Dennison certainly had that.

"There it is," Parmalee said.

They rode up to the general store and dismounted in front of it. As they were about to enter, several men converged on them with guns drawn.

"What the hell—" Parmalee began.

"Stand fast!" a man said. Parmalee noticed the badge on his shirt.

"Easy," Parmalee said to Ted.

"What's going on?"

"Just take it easy."

"Shut up!" the sheriff snapped nervously. The hand he was holding his gun in was shaking.

"Sheriff, take it easy," Parmalee said. "Nobody's trying nothing. Just you and your boys be calm."

"Take their guns!" the sheriff said.

No one moved. Parmalee looked around at them, and they were all sort of eyeing each other, each waiting for the other to move. From the way they looked, they were all storekeepers. One nervous lawman, and a handful of store clerks.

"Sheriff," Parmalee said, "you'll have to tell them *who* you want to take our guns."

The sheriff frowned. Parmalee knew his problem. There were five other men, and he had to pick one. It was a tough decision.

"Sheriff, you want to tell us what's going on?" Parmalee asked.

"As if you didn't know."

"Humor me," Parmalee said. "Pretend we don't."

"You killed her."

"Killed who?" Parmalee asked. Ted Shea felt a chill run down his spine. All they had done was ride into town, and they were being accused of murder. This was too crazy to believe.

"Killed who?" he repeated.

"Well, look at that," Walton said.

"Jesus," Hankman said. "If we wait long enough, maybe *they'll* shoot them."

"They're not gonna shoot them," Harry the Hat said.

They were standing down the street, watching what was taking place in front of the general store.

"Why not?" Hankman asked.

"Because that's the law," Harry the Hat said. "At least, one of them is."

"Which one?" Walton asked.

"The short, stocky one with the shaky hand. He just might plug one of them by accident."

"I wonder what it's all about?"

They had gotten to Dennison just about an hour before Parmalee and Ted Shea. Walton and Hankman had spent the time in a cafe, eating. Harry the Hat, on the other hand, had spent the time in the saloon. Consequently, he thought he *knew* what it was all about.

"There was a murder here yesterday."

"A murder?" Hankman said.

"Who?" Walton asked. "Who was killed?"

"A girl," Harry the Hat said. "A sixteen-year-old girl. She was raped, and beaten to death."

"How do you know that?" Hankman asked.

"Because I keep my ears open."

"And I don't?" Hankman was belligerent.

"You can't hear much in a hotel room."

"Hey, listen—"

"That's what I was doing," Harry the Hat said, and walked away.

"That guy gets on my nerves."

"As long as he coverin' your back, you got nothin' to worry about," Walton said.

"Look," Hankman said. "They ain't even taken their guns yet."

"Probably afraid to."

"Think they know who they got there?"

"No," Walton said, rubbing his jaw, "they got

them a couple of strangers, so they think they got a couple of killers."

"What do we do?" Hankman said.

"Whataya want to do? Go over there and take them away from the law?"

"We're supposed to kill Parmalee," Hankman said. "We can't do that if he's in jail."

Walton rubbed his jaw some more and then said, "Let's just watch and see what happens."

"You going to tell us who was killed?" Parmalee asked.

"What do we do, Sheriff?" one of the other men asked.

"How the hell do I know?" the sheriff answered. "The worse thing I ever had to deal with was some drunk. Handling killers is—"

"We didn't kill anyone," Ted Shea said. "What makes you think we did?"

Parmalee answered before the shaky lawman could. "We're strangers, Ted," he said. "That's all the reason these good citizens need."

"That's ridiculous," Ted said, looking around him at all the nervous men who were holding guns on him.

"All right," Parmalee said, turning to face the sheriff. He had to deal with the starpacker, because the others would follow his lead—for want of a real leader, that is. "Either put the gun up, or start pulling the trigger."

"Wha—what?" The sheriff started to blink his eyes rapidly.

"Mr. Shea and I are driving a herd of cows from

Montana to Kansas. We stopped outside of town and came in for some supplies. We haven't killed anyone."

"You say."

Parmalee turned and looked at the storekeeper who had spoken. The man, fortyish and potbellied, widened his eyes as Parmalee stepped his way and didn't stop until the barrel of the man's gun was pressed against Parmalee's belly.

"You pull the trigger," Parmalee said.

The man was making an effort not to blink, and as a result his eyes were starting to water.

"Come on," Parmalee urged. He put his hand on the man's gun and pressed it tighter against him. "Pull the trigger or let the gun go."

The man tried to look past Parmalee to the sheriff, but the lawman had found something else to look at. Finally, the man released his hold on the gun, and Parmalee took it from him.

Parmalee then turned quickly and snatched the sheriff's gun from his hand.

"Hey!" the lawman complained.

Parmalee looked at the rest of the "posse" and said, "Give it up, boys. This is not your line of work."

The others stared at him, then slowly holstered their guns—or tucked them into their belts—and walked away.

"You, too," Parmalee said to the man whose gun he had taken.

"My gun."

"It'll be at the sheriff's office. You can pick it up later."

The man hesitated, then wilted beneath Parmalee's stare and walked away.

"Now," Parmalee said, facing Ted Shea and the sheriff, "Ted, you go in and buy your supplies."

"What are you gonna do?"

He clapped his right hand on the sheriff's shoulder, causing the man to jump, and said, "The sheriff and I are going to go to his office and have a little talk." Parmalee looked at the lawman and said, "Aren't we, Sheriff?"

The sheriff swallowed hard. "Uh, s-sure, Mister—"

"Parmalee, Sheriff," Parmalee said, "the name is Parmalee."

The sheriff swallowed again, harder this time, and said, "Parmalee?"

Parmalee gave the man a cold smile. "Let's go to your office."

Hankman and Walton watched as Parmalee and the sheriff walked across the street to the sheriff's office. As they entered, Hankman turned to face his companion.

"So what do we do now, Walt? Parmalee's goin' to jail. We sure as hell can't get to him in there."

"No, he ain't goin' to jail."

"Whataya talkin' about, he ain't goin' to jail, Walt?" Hankman asked. "You just seen him go into the sheriff's office just as plain as I did." Hankman enunciated very carefully, trying to make his point. "The sheriff ... took ... him ... to ... jail."

"You're watchin', Hank," Walton said, "but you

ain't seein'. Parmalee just took the sheriff to his office."

"What's the difference?"

"Just keep watchin'," Walton said, "and you'll see the difference."

CHAPTER TWENTY-ONE

After they entered the sheriff's office, Parmalee tossed two guns on the desk, the sheriff's and the other man's. The sheriff stood in the center of the room, unsure of what to do.

"Have a seat, Sheriff," Parmalee said.

The sheriff looked around.

"Behind your desk would be nice."

"Yeah, sure," the man said nervously.

The sheriff walked around and sat behind his desk. He started to reach for his gun, then thought better of it and pulled his hand back.

"Just leave it there for a while," Parmalee said.

The sheriff nodded.

Parmalee walked to the window, brushed aside the curtain and looked out. Down the street, the two men who had been watching them were still there, and still watching. It looked like Max Venable's men had been about to make their move when the sheriff and his men had stepped into it.

Parmalee thought about Ted Shea at the general store, and figured he was safe enough. Chances were good Venable's men were going to try for Parmalee first.

He turned and looked at the sheriff, who was almost cowering behind his desk. As ludicrous as it seemed, he and Ted Shea owed the man something.

"When was the girl killed?"

"Huh?" The sheriff started as Parmalee spoke to him.

"What's wrong with you?"

"I, uh, didn't know who you were when we, uh, drew down on you out there. I hope you—"

"Forget it," Parmalee said. "When was the girl killed?"

"Last night."

"I know that," Parmalee said patiently. "What time last night?"

"I don't know."

"Did you have a doctor look at the body?"

"Of course."

"What time did he say she was killed?"

"Oh, right," the lawman said. "Uh, she was found at first light, and the doctor said she'd been dead about three or four hours."

"Where was she found?"

"Behind the saloon."

"Good," Parmalee said. "What time do the saloons close in this town?"

"We only got one."

"What time does it close?"

"Two."

"Did it close on time last night?"

The man hesitated, then admitted, "I don't know."

"Check it out," Parmalee said. "And then find out who left at closing time. That'll give you a list of suspects to check out."

"Are you a detective?" the sheriff asked, frowning.

"I worked for Pinkerton once," Parmalee said.

"Why are you helping me, after what we did to you and your friend?"

Parmalee opened the door and said, "Maybe this'll keep you from jumping on any more strangers."

"I tried to say I was sorry about that."

"I know you did," Parmalee said. "We're lucky you're able to make that apology."

"I know, I know," the sheriff said, "you could have been killed out there."

"Funny," Parmalee said, "I was thinking the same thing about you."

As Ted Shea was leaving the general store, Parmalee stepped up onto the boardwalk.

"Down the street, two men," Parmalee said. "Take a look without turning your head."

Ted Shea did as he was told.

"Know them?" Parmalee asked.

"No. Why?"

"They're real interested in us."

"You think they work for Max?"

"I think he imported some talent, and they've been on our trail."

"Why have they waited a month?"

"My guess is that when something happens,

it's supposed to happen far away from Max Venable's backyard. They were probably ready to make a move when the sheriff and his men got in the way."

"There's nothing stopping them now."

"Unless there's somebody missing."

"You mean there's more than two?"

"That's my guess," Parmalee said. "I think I remember seeing three of them when we rode in."

"So where's the other one?"

"They're probably wondering the same thing."

"Where the hell is Ross?" Hankman asked.

"I don't know. Maybe he's at the saloon."

"Or the whorehouse," Hankman said. "Wherever he is, we're gonna miss our chance unless we move now."

"Take Parmalee without Ross?" Walton asked. "You really want to do that?"

Hankman made a face and said, "No."

They watched as Parmalee and Ted Shea mounted up and started out of town.

"We missed our chance," Hankman said in disgust.

Walton clapped him on the shoulder. "There will be another one. Let's go and find Harry the Hat."

When the two men reached the herd, Laura and Joey moved away from the wagon to meet them.

"Any trouble?" Laura asked.

Parmalee and Ted dismounted and exchanged a glance.

"I'll tell you about it later," Ted said. He turned to Parmalee and asked, "Did they follow us?"

"No," Parmalee said, "but they don't have to. We're not going to be hard to find."

"Hard to find for who?" Laura asked. "What's going on here?"

Ted looked at Parmalee, who nodded.

"Come on, Laura," he said. "Help me stow these supplies."

As Ted walked away with Laura, explaining everything to her, Parmalee turned to Joey.

"You want to help me unsaddle these horses and rub them down?"

"We gonna camp here for the night?"

"That's the idea."

"Can I stand watch?"

Parmalee looked at her and said, "Let's talk about that after we take care of the horses."

CHAPTER TWENTY-TWO

DAY THIRTY-FIVE: "Crossed a river today. Lost a calf and its mother when the mother went to help it. Joey cried. Laura wondered if we could butcher the beef under water. That surprised me. Laura's changed; I just can't figure if it's a change for the better or worse. She's stronger, but she's colder. Is that better? Parmalee is cold, but he seems to be paying more attention to Joey."

DAY THIRTY-SIX: "I asked Parmalee if we were being followed. I can't tell. I don't know how he can. He says they are there. I asked him what they are waiting for. He's an odd man. He admitted that he didn't know. I didn't think a man like him would admit that. Maybe I don't really know what kind of man he is. I admit to myself here that I never expected him to still be with us after thirty-six days—or even six. I thought he'd pull out. I was wrong about him. I'm glad."

DAY THIRTY-NINE: "Parmalee says we have another problem. Indians. He says they're Pawnee, and they've been watching us. He says they're not violent by nature, and we may just have to trade with them. I thought all Indians were violent by nature. I'm learning new things from Parmalee."

On the night of the fortieth day, they camped near a river. Parmalee told Joey that she could stand first watch with him. Laura didn't want her to.

"She needs her rest," Laura argued.

"We may have to use her for this," Parmalee said, looking at Ted.

Laura looked at Ted, who just shrugged. She shook her head, clearly unhappy with the support she was getting from her husband, and walked away. Laura climbed into the back of the wagon, where she slept each night. Joey usually slept underneath the wagon.

"We'll wake you for second watch," Parmalee said to Ted.

"Maybe I better go and talk to Laura."

"Why don't you leave her alone?" Parmalee asked. "You might just make things worse."

After a moment, Ted said, "Yeah, maybe you're right. Good night. Good night, Joey."

" 'Night, Daddy."

As Ted walked off, Joey said, "Tell me about the Indians."

Hankman, Walton and Ross were camped a few miles behind the herd.

"I say we go and get them tomorrow," Hankman said. "What do you say?" He was talking to Walton, but Harry the Hat Ross answered.

"We should take it easy."

"Take it easy?" Hankman said. "If it wasn't for you and your whores, this job would be done by now."

Harry the Hat was brushing the brim of his hat and was not looking at Hankman.

"If the job didn't get done in Dennison, then it wasn't supposed to get done."

"That's a load of crap."

"Hank—"

Hankman held his hand up to Walton to quiet him. "Whataya think, Walt? You think Harry the Hat may be a little scared of Parmalee?"

Walton sucked in his breath and watched Ross. For a few seconds Harry the Hat Ross didn't move, and when he did, it was to set his hat down gently. Only when he was sure his hat was settled on his saddlebags and not in danger of falling into the dirt did he look at Hankman.

"Let's get one thing straight," he said. "Walt called me in on this because he knew that neither of you could take Parmalee."

"What a—"

"Don't bother arguing," Ross said. "Ask Walt and he'll tell you it's so."

Hankman looked at Walton, whose gaze wandered away.

"So does that put you in charge?" Hankman demanded.

"No," Ross said, "but it does give me some say in when and where I'll take Parmalee down."

"And when is that going to be?" Hankman

asked. He leaned forward, picked up a cup and poured himself some coffee.

"Well, it sure as hell ain't gonna be while we're in the middle of a bunch of Indians."

"Indians?" Hankman said, looking at Walton. "Who said anything about Indians?"

"They're just Pawnee," Walton said.

"Whataya talkin' about, just Pawnee?" Hankman said. "Indians are Indians. They're all murderin', thievin' savages . . . ain't they?"

"Not the Pawnee," Walton assured.

"Still," Harry the Hat said, "they're all around us, watching us and the Shea herd."

Hankman looked around but could see nothing but darkness. "What are we supposed to do then?"

"We'll wait," Ross said.

"For what?"

"For the Indians to make a move . . . or not."

"What if they don't?" Hankman asked.

"Then we'll just keep goin'," Ross said. "I think I'll wait until they reach Kansas."

Walton spoke this time. "The old man wants Parmalee dead before then," he said. "If they get that far with the herd, Shea might be able to get it to the railhead without him."

"Once they reach Kansas, they'll still have better than two hundred miles to make," Ross said. "Shea will never get there without Parmalee."

"But the old man—" Walton began.

"The old man isn't here," Harry the Hat cut him off. With that, he picked up his hat and began brushing the brim again, trying to clean off some imagined smudge.

Walton poured himself a cup of coffee and wondered how he was going to explain this to the old man, and to Rex Cameron. Cameron was supposed to have been with them, but the first time Cameron had gone into a town to send a telegram, he had been called back to the ranch on some kind of urgent business. He had told Walton that he would try to catch up with them if they hadn't returned by the time his business was finished. Both Cameron and Old Man Venable were probably wondering what was taking so long.

Walton wouldn't admit it to anyone—not even Hankman—but he was glad that Ross wanted to take Parmalee himself. Walton wanted no part of Parmalee face to face, but if Ross didn't get the job done soon, Walton was going to have to get his rifle out and take care of Parmalee the way he had killed many men in the past—with a bullet in the back.

If Harry the Hat wasn't able to handle Parmalee, Walton might end up doing that anyway.

Hankman huddled in his blanket, afraid to close his eyes for fear some Indian would sneak into camp and take his scalp. God, how he hated Indians! They scared the shit out of him.

"So, if the Pawnee are not warlike," Joey said, after Parmalee had told her about them, "why are we afraid of them?"

"We're not afraid of them, Joey," Parmalee said. "We're wary of them."

"What does that mean?" she asked. "Wary?"

"It means we'll be real careful around them."

"Why?"

"Because there is violence in all of us," Parmalee explained.

"Even me?"

"Even you," he said. "What would you do if someone tried to hurt your mother or father?"

"I'd hurt them first." She said it without any hesitation.

"See?"

"But we're not gonna try and hurt the Pawnee."

He leaned toward her and said in a low voice, "Let's hope they don't think we are."

"Then, if we don't try to hurt them, they'll let us pass."

"That depends on how hungry they are," Parmalee said, sitting up straight again and speaking in a normal tone. "If the hunting has been bad for them, our beef is going to look mighty good."

"Then they might try to take the herd?"

"Another tribe might try to take it," Parmalee said, "like the Apaches or Comanches. The Pawnee, they'll probably try to trade for some first."

"And if they do?"

"Then we'll give them some."

"For free?"

"Well, I don't think we'll have much use for anything they could give us."

"Will Pa give them some cows? I mean, just give them away?"

"He will if he listens to me."

"He always listens to you."

Parmalee didn't comment on that.

"Ma, though, she don't."

"No," Parmalee said, "she doesn't."

"I don't think Ma likes you."

"That's okay."

"Do you like her?"

"What?"

"She's real pretty," Joey said. "When we go into town, I see men watchin' her."

"Men'll be watching you like that when you grow up."

"I hope not."

"Why not?"

"Ma says they're animals."

"All men?"

Joey thought a moment, then said, "Well . . . pretty near."

Parmalee hesitated a moment. "Well, you listen to what your mother says until you're old enough to form your own opinions."

"I have my own opinions now."

"You do?"

"Uh-huh," she said. "I don't think my pa is an animal, so it can't be all men, right?"

"Right."

They sat in silence for a few moments, and then Joey put her hand on his arm. He looked down at her.

"I don't think you're an animal, Parmalee."

The look in her eyes as she stared up at him made him very uncomfortable.

"Uh, well, thanks, Joey," he finally stammered. "Look, why don't you go and get some sleep now?"

"But—"

"No buts," he said. "Remember you said your pa listens to what I say? Did he tell you why?"

"He says you know what you're doin'," she replied. "He says that if we get this herd through, it's gonna be because of you, and he couldn't pay you enough for that."

"Yeah, well, if he listens, you should listen, too, right?"

"I guess." She stood up and said, "G'night, Parmalee."

" 'Night."

She started to walk away, then turned back and said, "Of course, Ma don't agree with him. I mean, about not bein' able to pay you enough. 'Night."

As she hurried to her bed under the wagon, Parmalee thought to himself that it would take a hell of a lot to make Laura Shea agree with him on anything.

CHAPTER TWENTY-THREE

Hankman woke to someone kicking him.

"What the hell—" he said, coming awake. He looked up and saw Walton standing above him.

"Get up, Hank," he said. "We got company."

"What? Who?" Hankman sat up, blinking at the sun and looking around. What he saw froze his blood.

The camp was filled with Indians.

"Parmalee."

Parmalee opened his eyes immediately and looked at Ted Shea. He knew that Ted had only called his name once.

"What?"

"Look."

Parmalee sat up and looked where Ted was pointing. Up on a hill, looking down at them while in plain sight, were about half a dozen Indians.

"Pawnee?" Ted asked.

Parmalee squinted to get a better look and then nodded his head. "Yeah," he said, getting to his feet.

"What do we do?"

"We wait."

"For what?"

"For them to make the first move."

"And then what?"

Parmalee looked at Ted and saw the tension in the set of his jaw. He glanced around and saw that Laura and Joey were still asleep.

"Ted," he said, "if and when they ride down here, I don't want to see your hand anywhere near a gun."

"But—"

"If there's going to be gunplay, I'll handle it."

"Against six of them?"

"Just do as I say," Parmalee ordered. "Now, go and wake your family. Make sure Laura knows what I just said. I don't want to see that rifle in her hands. Got it?"

"Yeah, yeah, I got it," Ted said.

"Take a deep breath and relax, Ted," Parmalee said. "Just relax."

Ted Shea walked away to wake his wife and daughter, and Parmalee looked up at the Indians. Two . . . no, three of them had rifles. Those were the three he'd have to watch the closest. The others had either bows and arrows or lances; they'd have to make an obvious move if violence was their intent. Those with guns would have the rifles across their arms, and could easily pull the trigger without warning.

He'd have to watch them very closely.

* * *

Hankman stood up alongside Walton and Harry the Hat Ross. Walton stood stiffly, but Hankman was fidgeting, his hand hovering dangerously close to his gun.

"You touch that gun," Harry the Hat said in a low voice, "and I'll shove it all the way up your ass and pull the trigger."

"What the hell—"

"Just stand quiet," Ross said, "and let me handle this."

"You don't—"

"Shut up, Hank," Walton said.

"Who does he think—"

"Shut up!"

Hank fell silent, but he wasn't about to let some Indian lift his scalp. If one of those savages came anywhere near him, he was going to put a hole in him.

"Stay here," Ross said to both of them, and walked toward a brave who looked to be in charge.

Parmalee heard Ted Shea, Laura and Joey come up behind him. Joey stood very close to Parmalee and looked up the hill.

"Are they gonna kill us?" she asked.

"No, Joey," Parmalee said. "Remember what I told you last night?"

"I remember."

Joey slid her hand into Parmalee's left. He didn't know what to do about it, so he just held it. If she had tried to take his right hand, he would have had to tell her no.

"Maybe if we fire a shot—" Laura started.

"No guns," Parmalee said.

"These are Indians," Laura said, "savages. My father always said the only way to deal with them was by force—"

Parmalee turned on her. "Is your father a great Indian fighter, now?"

She flinched and stared at him, shocked into silence for the moment.

"Uh, no, but he had some experience—"

"Forget about Max Venable's experience with Indians," Parmalee said. "These are not people you can buy with money. Understand?"

"Sure," Laura relented after a moment, "I understand."

"Then shut up and do as you're told."

"Parmalee, listen—" Ted started, but Parmalee cut him off.

"That goes for you, too. This is one of the things you hired me for, Ted. Let me do what I'm being paid to do, okay?"

Ted and Laura stared at Parmalee. The next voice was Joey's.

"Here they come," she said.

Hankman and Walton watched nervously as Harry Ross spoke with the brave in command. There were eight other Pawnee braves in camp, and they were keeping a wary eye on Hankman and Walton.

"I don't like this," Hankman complained.

"What do you want to do about it?"

"Let's shoot our way out of here," Hankman said. "Only half of them have rifles. We'll take them out first."

Walton was thinking about it.

"Come on, Walt."

Hankman's gun hand was flexing and unflexing. Walton was about to okay the move when Ross turned around and started walking back.

"Wait, Hank," Walton said. "Wait."

"Stay here," Parmalee said. He released Joey's hand and moved forward on foot to meet the six approaching Pawnee braves.

"What does he think he's doing?" Laura asked.

"He's right, Laura. He's doing what we're paying him to do."

"I'm gonna go and get my rifle."

Ted grabbed her by the wrist and held her tightly. "Stay here, Laura!" he hissed.

They watched while Parmalee conversed with one of the braves. His name was Sleeping Dog, and he spoke English well enough for Parmalee to understand.

"My people are hungry," Sleeping Dog said, "and you have many cows."

"Sleeping Dog," Parmalee said, "it would be our honor to help your people get something to eat."

"We can trade."

"There is no need to trade," Parmalee said. "We will make a gift of . . . two cows."

"I have many hungry mouths, many empty bellies. The hunting has not been good."

"All right," Parmalee said, holding up four fingers. "Four cows."

Sleeping Dog turned and looked back at the other five braves. Parmalee did not see any of them communicate anything to the brave, so he knew this was just a ruse of some sort on the part of Sleeping Dog.

"Six cows," the brave finally said. He held up five fingers of one hand, and the thumb on the other. Parmalee watched the three braves who were armed with rifles. Their eyes were on him.

Parmalee hesitated, making it seem as though he were thinking about it, then held up five fingers. "Five cows."

Now Sleeping Dog took a few moments before nodding and saying, "Five."

"Wait," Parmalee said, holding both hands up, palms out. He walked back to the Sheas and said to Ted, "We're going to give him five cows."

"What?" Laura asked. "We're just gonna give him five cows, for nothing?"

Parmalee looked at her and said, "Let's call it a toll, for safe passage."

"Ted—" Laura said, looking at her husband.

"Parmalee," Ted Shea said, "that's a little steep, isn't it? I mean, you said they weren't violent."

"They're hungry," Parmalee said. "That makes them even more dangerous than if they were violent by nature."

They stood silently for a few moments, and then Parmalee said, "It's your herd, Ted. That makes it your call."

"What do they want?" Walton asked.

"Food," Ross replied.

"We don't have any food to give them," Hankman said.

"Sure we do," Ross said.

"What are you talkin' about?"

Ross looked at Hankman. "We're givin' them everything we have."

"What?"

Ross looked at Walton. "We can ride into any town and get more," he said. "They can't."

Walton thought a few seconds and then nodded. "It makes sense."

"Givin' our food to a bunch of savages makes sense to you?" Hankman asked.

"More sense than havin' them kill us for what we have," Walton answered. He looked at Ross. "Give it all to them."

Ross nodded, turned and walked away.

"If we have to stop for supplies," Hankman said, "that herd's gonna get farther ahead of us."

"We'll catch up."

"This is takin' too long," Hankman mumbled, shaking his head. "Too damned long."

Walton didn't want to say so, but he agreed with Hankman. This *was* takin' too damned long, and he thought he knew how to speed things up.

Parmalee and Ted walked five cows out to the Pawnee and watched as they herded them away. They had also thrown into the deal some of the supplies they had in their wagon. They were going to have to stop again to restock. Behind them they could both feel Laura's anger hanging in the air like a buzzard, waiting to drop down on one of them. Parmalee decided that it wasn't going to be him.

"You're going to have to deal with your wife," Parmalee said, "because I'm not."

"Don't worry about her."

"I'm not," Parmalee said, "but maybe you should."

Parmalee walked away before Ted could ask him what he meant.

CHAPTER TWENTY-FOUR

DAY FORTY-TWO: "Laura is still furious, but I don't know if she's madder at Parmalee for giving away five of our cows, or me for letting him do it. Tomorrow we'll camp outside of Kenicut, Nebraska, where we'll buy supplies, and by the next day we'll be in Colorado.

"I'm going into Kenicut alone for supplies. I don't want to take a chance on either the Indians or Max's men swooping down on Laura and Joey and the herd. Parmalee argued, but I decided that since I was paying him, I should have the last word. He seemed to respect that. God knows he doesn't respect me for much else."

Since Ted was going into town alone for supplies, they decided that he should take a packhorse. Parmalee untied one of the horses from the back of the wagon and outfitted it to carry supplies.

Parmalee was sort of surprised that the Pawnee had not tried to trade for a horse or two. To some Indians, horse meat was better than beef.

Parmalee handed the reins of the packhorse to Ted and warned, "Be careful. Watch your back trail both to town and back. If you get in trouble, fire some shots. If I hear them, I can come running."

"I'll be fine," Ted said.

"Be careful, Daddy," Joey said, looking up at her father with big, worried eyes.

"I will, baby. You be sure to do what Parmalee tells you, all right?"

"I will."

"And mind your mother."

Joey nodded, and Ted nudged his horse's ribs and rode off.

"He'll be all right, won't he?" Joey asked Parmalee.

"He'll be fine." Parmalee wished he was as sure as he sounded. "Come on," he said to her, "let's take a look at the herd."

Rex Cameron crossed a cold camp and figured he was about two days behind Walton and the other two. He couldn't understand why they hadn't returned yet, or why he hadn't crossed their path as they were on the way back. If he hadn't been called back to the ranch, he could have made sure the job was done by now. Either the men he had hired—Walton and the men *he* had picked—were too damned slow, or something had happened. Maybe they had made their try at Parmalee and had lost. If that was the case, Cameron didn't know what he would do, but he figured he might as well wait until that problem arose before he worried about it.

Riding day and night he had made good time, stopping twice in towns along the way for fresh horses. In a day and a half, maybe two days, he'd know what the situation was, and he would be able to telegraph the old man. It had been all he could do to keep Max Venable from jumping on a horse and coming with him, but the older man would have slowed him down, and the trip would probably have killed him.

He kicked at the cold ashes, then mounted up and continued on.

"I'm gonna stay on their trail while you fellas go and get some supplies," Walton said.

Harry the Hat thought that one over and nodded. "That makes sense."

Grudgingly, Hankman had to admit that it did. "Only why don't I follow them and you ride into town for supplies," he said to Walton, out of earshot of Harry Ross.

"I'm a better tracker than you are."

"Like hell."

"Just do it, Hank, okay?"

"I don't like Ross—"

"You don't have to like him, dammit!" Walton snapped. "Don't talk to each other; I don't care. Just get the supplies and catch up with me. It shouldn't take you more than a day."

And in that day, Walton had decided that he'd take care of Parmalee in his own way—from a hundred yards off, with a rifle, in the back. By the time Ross and Hankman caught up to him, the damned job would be done.

He hadn't really needed two more men along, anyway—especially two like Hankman, who was always complaining, and Ross, who was always cleaning that damned hat.

Funny, he'd worked with Harry the Hat before, and the damned hat never bothered him as much as it did on this trip.

As Ross and Hankman mounted up to leave, Hankman said to Walton, "What's the name of this town, anyway?"

"Kenicut," Walton said. "You shouldn't run into any trouble at all."

When Ted Shea rode into Kenicut, the greeting he and Parmalee had gotten in Dennison came to mind. This time, alone, he'd keep a keen eye out for trouble.

He rode up to the front of the general store, dismounted and went inside.

Moments later Hankman and Harry the Hat rode into Kenicut. They were unimpressed with the town. They hadn't spoken a word to each other all the way, and that didn't change until they were approaching the general store.

"You go and get the supplies," Ross said.

"Why? Where are you goin'?"

Ross gave Hankman a hard stare and said, "None of your business."

"Hey," Hankman called after him, "we ain't supposed to hang around here longer than it takes to stock up."

Ross, riding away, called over his shoulder, "I'll meet you right here in an hour."

"An hour? But—" It was no use. There was no talking to Ross, and when Hankman thought about it, he'd just as soon split up, anyway.

He rode his horse to the general store, dismounted and started to step up onto the boardwalk when he spotted Ted Shea's horse. He knew it by the "TS" brand. He looked around, but there was only the one horse bearing that brand. He wondered, then, who was inside the store, Parmalee or Shea himself.

It didn't really matter. This was too good a chance to pass up. He slid his gun in and out of its holster a few times, to make sure it wouldn't stick, and then stepped over to the side. Whichever one of them came out of the general store had a big surprise coming.

Lyle Conagher was passing on the other side of the street when he saw a man skulking around in front of the general store. He frowned. Conagher was a man who knew trouble when he saw it brewing. He'd had enough of it over his thirty-two years, the last six of which had been spent making his living gambling. Before that he had worked many different jobs, and had found many different kinds of trouble. The form it usually came in was either female or cards.

The man across the street was planning what looked like an ambush, and Lyle Conagher had never before stood by and watched one man shoot another from ambush. It just didn't sit right with him.

He crossed over so that when he arrived on the other side, he was behind the man. He took out a lucifer stick, put it in his mouth, and chewed on it while he waited to see what was going to develop.

CHAPTER TWENTY-FIVE

Preston Walton looked down on the Shea camp. He saw Parmalee and the two females, the mother and daughter. He had seen Ted Shea leave earlier with a packhorse. Obviously, Shea was going to town for supplies. Walton wondered if Shea would cross trails with Hankman and Ross. If he did, Hankman might just be fool enough to kill him. Hopefully, Ross would be able to keep that from happening. Old Man Venable wouldn't like it if his son-in-law was killed—at least, not until he okayed it.

He looked around for a likely spot to take his shot from. There was a cluster of rocks above the camp, across from where he was now, that would afford him a perfect vantage point. The shot would be one of only about thirty yards, and he made those kinds of shots in his sleep.

He took his rifle out, held it lightly in his hands for a moment, then slid it back into its scabbard.

He pulled his horse's head around and started to ride around the camp to those rocks.

Harry the Hat set his hat down carefully on top of the dresser, then turned and looked at the woman reclining nude on the bed.

"How do you want it, honey?" she asked. "Fast, or slow?"

She was dark-haired, in her thirties, with the kind of firm body Ross liked: heavy breasts, meaty thighs, and a dark, tangly bush between her legs.

"I'd like to go slow, darlin'," he said, "I just don't have the time."

"All right, then," she said, moving her legs. . . .

Ted Shea paid for his supplies, picked them up in both arms and started to leave the store. He was totally unaware of the fact that had Parmalee come alone, he would have made two trips in and out of the store, in order to keep one hand free at all times—his gun hand.

As he left the store, he heard something to his left, turned and saw a man pointing a gun at him.

"Wha—"

"Shea?"

"That's right," Ted said, and then he recognized the man as one of the men from Dennison. "You were watching us in Dennison."

"That's right."

"You work for my father-in-law?"

"Right again."

Ted frowned. "I can't believe Max wants me dead."

"He wants you stopped," Hankman said. "I'm gettin' tired of waitin', so I'm gonna do it this way."

"Wait—"

"Sorry."

Hankman extended his arm, and as he did, Ted saw the man behind him lift his gun and bring the barrel down across the back of Hankman's head. The man fell like a sack of grain and didn't make a sound.

"Thanks."

"What's this fella's beef with you?" the other man asked.

"That'll take some explaining," Ted said. "You'd better come with me."

"I've got some things at the hotel."

"Get them," Ted said. "I've got a camp and a herd just outside of town. When this man wakes up, he and his friends aren't gonna be too happy."

"Well," the man said, frowning, "I was tired of this town, anyway."

"Good," Ted said. "I'll have a meal and an explanation waiting for you."

Conagher shook his head slightly, wondering why he always managed to get himself into trouble.

"I'll meet you there," Conagher said. He looked down at Hankman and added, "What do you want to do about this unpleasant fella?"

"Leave him."

"We could go to the sheriff."

"It's not worth it," Ted said. "I'll explain it all later."

"All right," Conagher said, "it's your call. I'll go to the hotel and check out."

As the man started to walk away Ted called out, "What's your name?"

"Conagher."

"Shea."

Conagher waved and said, "See you later, Shea."

Ted tied the supplies to the back of the packhorse, mounted up and looked down at the fallen man who had been hired by Max Venable. Whether or not Max had ordered it, the man had been about to kill him.

The remainder of the trip was going to be more dangerous than it had been so far, if the men for hire had decided that killing him was the only way to stop him.

Suddenly, Ted was even more glad for Parmalee's presence than he had been up to now.

Twenty minutes later, Lyle Conagher rode his horse from the livery and headed down the main street to the end of town. As he did so, he saw a man staggering across the street, holding his hand to the back of his head. It would have been very easy to put a bullet in the man. At the time he didn't really see a reason to.

Later, he would remember the opportunity.

Thirty minutes after that, Harry the Hat left the whorehouse and found Felix Hankman sitting on the boardwalk outside, holding the back of his head.

"What happened to you?" Ross asked. "You get robbed?"

"I ran into Shea," Hankman said. "I was talkin' to him when somebody hit me from behind."

"Parmalee?"

"I didn't see him," Hackman said, "and I didn't see Parmalee's horse, just Shea's and a packhorse."

"If they stopped for supplies so soon after Dennison," Ross said, "they must have run into the Pawnee, too."

Hankman didn't reply, and continued to rub the back of his head.

"You need a doctor?"

"No," Hankman said, "it's just a bump."

"Did you get the supplies?" Ross asked.

"No," Hankman said, "this happened before."

"You shouldn't have approached him without me."

Hankman gave Ross a sour look. "You was busy with somethin' else."

Ross ignored the comment. "Come on, let's get the supplies and meet up with Walton."

"Ain't you gonna make some kind of comment?" Hankman asked.

Ross reached down to help Hankman to his feet and said, "No."

Walton spread himself out over a long, flat rock and peered down at the camp. The rock was hot, pleasantly so against his body. The sun was high, but it was to his back and would not interfere with his shot. He pressed the rifle to his shoulder and sighted down the barrel. Parmalee was near the wagon, talking to the woman. When he moved away, out into the clear, Walton would wait for his back, and fire.

* * *

"What is this?" Laura asked. "For a man who murders for a living, you're pretty moral, aren't you?"

"You're a lovely woman, Laura," Parmalee said. "I've told you that before."

"Never mind that," she said. "All I'm askin' you for is something physical, something I can't—or haven't been able to—get from my husband."

"Your daughter is here."

"She's out by the herd."

He stared at her. "You don't quit, do you?"

"Not when I want something."

Parmalee hesitated, then said, "You don't want me; you just want a man."

"Right now," she said, "it's the same thing."

He looked down at the ground for a long moment . . . so long that she was about to say something when he looked at her.

"Stay near the wagon and don't move."

"Why? What is it?"

"Somebody's watching us."

"Indians again?"

"No."

"Who? My father's men?"

"Probably," Parmalee said. "I've got to go and get Joey. I'll bring her back here."

"Parmalee—" she said as he started to turn away.

"Laura," he said, looking at her hard, "don't move away from the wagon."

CHAPTER TWENTY-SIX

Parmalee knew he was at extremely high risk. He had to get Joey in; but as soon as he stepped away from the wagon, the man on the rock might open fire—and if the man was a backshooter, he wouldn't even wait until Parmalee turned around. Still, that little girl was out there all alone.

Laura Shea watched as Parmalee moved away from the wagon. He never once looked around, or up, or gave any indication as to where the man with the gun was. She looked around, but could not spot him. She was impressed by the fact that Parmalee seemed to be putting himself at risk out in the open because he was concerned for Joey.

Laura climbed into the wagon and retrieved her rifle. If and when someone took a shot at Parmalee, she wanted to be ready to return fire.

* * *

Walton watched as Parmalee moved away from the wagon and started walking toward his horse. Beyond the camp, Walton could see the herd, and a rider who had to be the little girl. Parmalee was probably riding out to relieve her. As Parmalee was mounting up, his back would make a perfect target.

He sighted down the barrel of the rifle and waited.

The way Parmalee figured it, the gunman's best shot would be as he was mounting up. His timing was going to have to be just right, and it might cost him a horse, but. . . .

He fitted his left foot into the stirrup, but instead of lifting he pushed off, throwing himself to the left. As he did, he grabbed his rifle just as the man fired. He rolled on the ground, listening to the bullet strike his saddle, but he didn't have time to check and see if the horse was hurt.

Laura heard the shot and saw Parmalee go down. She pinpointed where the shot had come from, aimed and fired hastily. She missed the man, but struck the rock, causing the man to duck down.

Parmalee rolled a little farther and came up on one knee ready to fire. Unfortunately, Laura had fired first and driven the man to cover.

Parmalee got to his feet and ran to where Laura was standing.

"I missed," she said.

"I know," he said. "Go and get Joey and bring her back here. Then you both stay near the wagon. Understand?"

"I understand. . . . Where are you going?"

"Just wait here!"

Laura didn't have to go looking for Joey. At the sound of the shot, Joey started to ride back to camp. Laura met her riding in.

"What happened?"

"Someone shot at Parmalee."

Joey dismounted. "Where is he?"

"He went up there," Laura said, pointing. "Come on, we have to get back to the wagon."

"Was he hurt, Mama?"

Laura thought a moment and then said, "I don't know, Joey."

As Laura Shea's bullet glanced off the rock, it threw some stone fragments into Walton's face, and he ducked away. He felt the sting on his face, and the panic in his chest. He was alone, and he had missed. Parmalee would be on his way up here, and Walton knew he couldn't take Parmalee *mano a mano*.

He ran to his horse, mounted and rode away as fast as he could. He had to join up with Hankman and Harry the Hat Ross.

It took Parmalee some time on foot to reach the point where the gunman had been. He could see the man's heel marks on the stone, and even found where Laura's bullet had impacted. The man had obviously fired just that once and then ridden away. If Laura hadn't fired at him and driven him away, Parmalee might have gotten off a more accurate shot than she had.

When Parmalee returned to camp, Joey came running out of the wagon to meet him.

"Are you all right, Parmalee?"

"Yes, I'm fine." He kept walking toward the wagon.

"Did you see him?"

"No," he said, "I didn't see him."

When he reached the wagon, Laura had climbed down.

"Damn it, woman!" he said. "Why can't you do as you're told?"

Laura recoiled, not so much from the words, but from the anger in his tone. She regained her composure quickly, though. "I like that. I save your life and this is the thanks I get?"

"You didn't save my life," he said, "you helped that man get away."

"What the hell are you talking about?"

"I was prepared for his shot," Parmalee explained, "and I was ready to return fire. Your shot made that impossible."

"I was trying to help you."

"You could have helped by staying near the wagon as I told you. If you had, the man would probably be dead by now."

"You would have gotten him where I missed, is that it?" she demanded.

"That's exactly it," he said. "I wouldn't have missed."

She glared at him, then turned and climbed back into the wagon.

"She was only tryin' to help, Parmalee," Joey said reasonably.

Parmalee stared down at her. "I know, Joey, I

know, but what you all have to understand is that the best way to help me is to do as I tell you. Do you understand?"

"Sure, Parmalee," Joey said, "I understand."

"Well," he said, "maybe you can explain it to your mother."

While Laura and Joey talked inside the wagon, Parmalee checked his horse. He had a bullet hole in his saddle, but the animal was all right. Parmalee took out his knife, pried the bullet free and dropped it on the ground. He mounted up then and rode out to the herd, thinking about Laura Shea. Maybe he had been hard on her, but that seemed to be the only way to get her to listen—if even *that* would work.

Somehow he doubted it.

CHAPTER TWENTY-SEVEN

When Ted Shea rode back into camp, Laura approached him and immediately told him what had happened.

"Are you and Joey all right?"

"We're fine."

"Did Parmalee get the man?"

"No."

"Is he all right?"

"He's fine. He's out by the herd."

Ted decided not to tell Laura what had happened in town—at least, not until he had told Parmalee. Once Lyle Conagher arrived in camp, there wouldn't be any way to keep it from her.

"I'll be right back," he said. "I have to talk to Parmalee."

"Ted, he yelled at me—"

"I'll talk to him, Laura," Ted promised. "Meanwhile, get the supplies put away, huh? You and Joey?"

"Sure."

He mounted up again and rode out to the herd.

Parmalee saw Ted riding out to him and turned his horse to face him.

"Laura told me what happened."

"They're all right."

"I know," Ted said. "Laura was pretty mad. What really happened?"

"She tried to help," Parmalee explained, "and the shooter got away."

Ted looked away, then back at Parmalee.

"Never mind," Parmalee said, staring at Ted. "You've got something to tell me."

"Yeah," Ted said, "how'd you know?"

"Never mind," Parmalee said again. "What happened in town?"

Quickly, Ted told Parmalee what had happened to him in town.

"You and this other fella . . ."

"Conagher."

"Yeah, Conagher," Parmalee said, "you didn't kill the other fella?"

Ted stared at Parmalee. "No. We left him there, unconscious."

Parmalee didn't comment. He looked out over the herd.

"What would you have done?"

"Killed him," Parmalee said.

"Why? It wasn't necessary."

Parmalee looked back at Ted. "It would have simplified matters," he said. "It would have given us one less to deal with, and it would have sent a message to the others."

"You'd kill a man to send a message?"

"When is this Conagher supposed to come?"

"He's probably right behind me."

"It wasn't such a good idea to invite him to camp," Parmalee said.

"He saved my life."

"Yeah. . . ."

"What? You think he was working with them?"

"No," Parmalee said, "I just don't think it's wise to invite strangers into camp."

"I'd better get back to camp before he gets there," Ted said. "I want to tell Laura what happened in town myself."

"Go ahead," Parmalee said. "I'll be in soon."

Ted nodded, and turned his horse around. Parmalee shook his head as he watched the man ride away.

It didn't take Conagher long to find the herd, and the camp. As he rode in, he saw the two women removing supplies from a packhorse. As he got closer, he realized that it was one woman and one girl. Both were pretty, but the young one was too young. The older one, though, was a handsome-looking woman, and well built. He realized there might be fringe benefits to having saved Ted Shea's life.

Laura stopped when she saw the man riding into camp. She reached into the wagon and brought out her rifle.

"Joey, get behind me."

As the man reined in his horse, Laura raised

the rifle, not pointing directly at him, but in his general direction.

"Hey, hold on, little lady," Conagher said, raising both his hands.

"What are you doin' here?" Laura demanded.

"I was invited."

"By who?"

"Ted Shea? You know him?"

"He's my husband."

Conagher felt a vague sense of loss. "Uh, do you mind if I put my hands down?" he asked, lowering them somewhat.

"Keep them up," Laura said, gesturing with the rifle. "Why would Ted invite you?"

Conagher put his hands back up and shrugged. "I helped him out of a jam in town."

"What kind of jam?"

Conagher noticed Ted Shea riding into camp and said, "Maybe he wants to tell you that himself."

Laura watched as her husband dismounted and walked over to them. "Put up the rifle, Laura," Ted said. "This is Conagher. He's a friend."

She lowered the rifle, but didn't put it down.

"He says there was some trouble in town."

"There was."

"When were you gonna tell me about it?" she asked angrily.

"That's what I was comin' to do now."

"Sure," she said, "after you talked to Parmalee first, right?"

"Laura—"

"Take care of your friend, Ted," she said. "Joey

and I have to finish putting the supplies in the wagon."

"Sure," Ted said, "go ahead."

"Come on, Joey."

Laura and Joey went back to what they were doing, and Ted approached Lyle Conagher.

"Your wife doesn't seem very happy about me being here," Conagher observed.

"Ah, it's not you," Ted said. "She's been through a lot. We've been on the trail almost two months."

"With trouble behind you?"

"Ah," Ted said, "sometimes, like today, it seems to be in front of us, too. Come on, unsaddle your horse. You're gonna stay for dinner."

"I don't know—"

"I do," Ted said. "I insist. I want you to meet Parmalee."

"I thought I heard your wife say that name," Conagher said. "Would that be Dan Parmalee?"

"Yes, that's him," Ted said. "Why, do you know Parmalee?"

Conagher looked thoughtful. "I did . . . once."

"Well, then," Ted said, "he'll be glad to see a friendly face."

"I don't know how glad he'll be to see me," Conagher said, "but it might be interesting to find out."

Just because Ted Shea had said "Conagher" didn't mean it had to be "Lyle" Conagher, but what were the chances that it wasn't? Parmalee wondered. He hadn't seen Lyle Conagher in a few years, but from Ted Shea's description, it certainly sounded like the gambler.

Although Parmalee and Conagher weren't exactly friends, they weren't enemies, either. Parmalee wasn't sure how he felt about seeing the man again, but the only way to find out was to go back into camp.

CHAPTER TWENTY-EIGHT

Parmalee waited until he could smell the coffee and bacon before riding into camp. As he arrived, he saw Ted and Conagher drinking coffee. Conagher spotted him as he was riding in and stood up.

Parmalee approached the fire. Ted poured a cup of coffee and Joey handed it to Parmalee.

"Thanks, Joey."

Ted stood back and watched the two men. From what Conagher had told him—and recalling that Parmalee had said nothing about knowing Conagher already—he was curious about how their meeting would go.

"Parmalee," Conagher said.

Parmalee looked Conagher up and down and said, "Long time, Lyle."

"A few years."

"You don't seem to have changed much."

"Not at all," Conagher said, "if I can help it."

"I understand you gave Mr. Shea here a hand in Kenicut."

"That's right."

"Why?"

"Parmalee—" Ted started.

"It's a fair question, Ted," Conagher said, cutting him off. "He looked like he was about to get bushwacked. I couldn't just stand by and watch."

"Food's ready," Laura called out.

Joey went to Laura, who ladled the food onto plates. Joey gave Ted a plate, then Parmalee, and finally Conagher. That done, she got one for herself.

"Joey," Laura called out, "come here and eat by me."

"But Ma—"

"Mind your mother," Ted said.

Joey sulked, but moved to the other side of the wagon to eat with her mother.

"I don't think anything was goin' to be said that she couldn't hear," Conagher said. "What's past is past, right, Parmalee?"

"That's what I've always felt," Parmalee said.

Ted frowned. Obviously something had happened between these two the last time they'd met; but neither was giving anything away, and he wasn't about to ask.

"What were you doing in Kenicut?" Parmalee asked Conagher.

"Passin' through," Conagher replied.

"Find a game there?"

"Not much," Conagher said. "Small stakes, too small for me."

"Well, you've bought into a high-stakes game now," Parmalee said.

"Ted was tellin' me about his father-in-law," Conagher said. "I've heard of Max Venable."

"Parmalee," Ted explained, "I thought Lyle might ride with us for a while."

"Ride with us," Parmalee said, looking at Conagher, "or work with us?"

"Well," Conagher said, "if I'm gonna come along, I might as well pull my weight. I've worked cows before . . . a long time ago, but I think I still remember how it's done."

"Why would you want to do that?" Parmalee asked.

"I might ask you the same question, Parmalee."

"I'm getting paid."

"Well," Conagher said, "I reckon I'll be headin' in the same direction, anyway. You mind if I ride along?"

"Hell no," Parmalee said, "we're going to be needing another gun. You *can* still use a gun, can't you?"

"Oh, yeah," Conagher said, "not as well as I can use a deck of cards, but I can use it."

"Good."

"Good," Conagher said.

Ted looked from one man to the other, and as the silence began to become oppressive, he asked, "Anyone want more coffee?"

When Hankman and Ross found Walton, he had a fire going and was drinking coffee. He had a look on his face that only Hankman had seen before.

Hankman and Ross told Walton what had happened in Kenicut, and Walton finally said, "That was stupid, Hank."

"Was it?" Hankman wanted to ask Walton what was on *his* mind, but didn't want to do it in front of Harry the Hat. "Maybe it was."

"Shea's not the one we were hired to take care of," Walton said.

"I thought we were hired to stop him from deliverin' his cows?" Hankman said.

"But not by killin' him."

"Well then, why don't we just ride on down there, kill Parmalee and get it over with."

"We can't afford to be seen," Walton said.

"We can wear masks."

Walton made a face and said, "I ain't never worn a mask in my life."

"Neither have I," Harry the Hat said.

"Besides," Walton said to Hankman, indicating Ross, "how you gonna get a mask over that hat?"

They decided to continue trailing the herd and wait for their opportunity.

"We'd better set a watch," Walton said.

"I'll take the first," Ross offered. "I've got to work on my hat."

That suited Hankman, and he agreed. Ross picked up his rifle and walked away from the fire, leaving Hankman and Walton to talk freely.

"Now that he's gone," Hankman said, "what the hell happened to you today:?"

"Whataya talkin' about?" Walton asked.

"Come on, Walt," Hankman said. "We've known each other a long time. Somethin' happened today."

Walton hesitated, then said, "Yeah, all right. I made a try for Parmalee today."

"What?" Hankman exclaimed. "You tried to shoot him in the back?" Hankman was well acquainted with Walton's way of doing things.

"I just wanted to get it over with."

"And?"

"I missed. He was ready for me. If it wasn't for Shea's wife, he might have gotten me. Hank, now I realize we really do have to wait for the right time and place."

"Yeah, sure," Hankman said, rubbing the lump on the back of his head. "I sure wish I knew who hit me on the head."

CHAPTER TWENTY-NINE

After dinner, Parmalee and Ted rode out to check the herd. Ted refused Conagher's offer to accompany them. For tonight, he said, Conagher was his guest. Tomorrow, if he wanted, he could start helping them. Conagher did not argue.

After Parmalee and Ted left camp, Conagher accepted Laura's offer of another cup of coffee. He was surprised when she sat down beside him.

"I suppose I should thank you," she said.

"For what?"

"For helping Ted."

"He's already thanked me."

"I know," she said, putting her hand on his arm, "but *I* should thank you, as well ... in my own way."

Conagher frowned and studied her face. There were some lines at the corners of her mouth, and she had work-hardened hands, but she was an extremely appealing-looking woman. She was full bodied, and the work that had ruined her hands had probably made her body strong and firm.

"Here?" he said.

"No," she said, "not here, but soon . . . if you're interested."

Conagher thought it over and decided that since he'd just met Ted Shea it wouldn't be like sleeping with the wife of a friend.

"Sure," he said, "I'm interested."

She smiled at him, squeezed his arm, and then got up and started cleaning up. Conagher couldn't help but wonder if she had made the same offer to Parmalee, and if he had taken it. If he had, maybe she wouldn't be making the offer to him.

He watched her as she walked back and forth, and found himself looking forward to the time when "soon" would come.

"What's going on between you and Conagher?" Ted asked when he and Parmalee reached the herd.

Parmalee didn't answer right away, and Ted thought he was going to have to ask him before he did; but he finally spoke.

"We're not exactly friends."

"I figured that out for myself," Ted said. "The question is, why? What happened?"

Parmalee looked at Ted. "I could tell you it's none of your business."

"A month ago I might have accepted that," Ted said, "but not now."

"No," Parmalee said. "You have changed some over the past month, haven't you?"

"I have, yes," Ted said, "and even more over the last couple of days. What I can't figure out is whether it's a change for the better, or the worse."

"I guess you'd have to ask your wife that."

"Why are you always making comments about Laura?" Ted asked.

"I get the impression that she's not a happy woman," Parmalee said.

"We could all be happier."

"How are things between you?"

Ted looked at Parmalee and said, "Now I could tell you it's none of your business—and you're changing the subject."

"I'll answer your question if you'll answer mine," Parmalee said.

"Deal," Ted agreed, "but since I asked first, you go first."

"All right," Parmalee said. "About three years ago, Conagher and I had a falling-out over a woman."

Ted waited, and when no more was forthcoming, he shrugged his shoulders and said, "That's it?"

"Isn't that enough?"

"Somehow I can't see you being upset over losing a woman."

"Maybe it was just losing her to Conagher," Parmalee said. "He's a slick, handsome, oily bastard, and he could probably have had any woman he wanted—but he wanted the one I had."

"I see."

"Now you," Parmalee said. "How are things between you and Laura?"

Ted hesitated, and looked as if he was searching for a word. When he finally found it, he let it slip out, as if he were reluctant to say it.

"Strained."

"To say the least?"

Ted looked at Parmalee and nodded. "This is my last chance, Parmalee," he said. "I know that. My last chance to keep my ranch, to keep my daughter, and to keep my wife."

"You think she'd go back to her father?"

Ted rubbed his jaw. "A year ago I would have said no. Five years ago I would have said it was unthinkable. Now. . . ."

Now, Parmalee thought. He wondered what Conagher and Laura were doing back in camp. Not much, probably, not with Joey around and either Parmalee or Ted due back in camp any minute. But Laura had made the offer to Parmalee, so what was to stop her from making it to Conagher? And if Parmalee knew Conagher, the man would be saying no, as he had.

"Well," Ted said, "one of us has to stay out here, and one of us has to go back to camp."

"I'll go back."

"All right," Ted said. "Relieve me in three hours."

"All right."

Parmalee pulled his horse around and rode back toward camp.

At the sound of the horse, Conagher looked away from Laura to see who was returning. It was Parmalee, and he wasn't surprised. They had some talking to do just between them.

Parmalee dismounted and handed the reins of his horse to Joey, who walked the horse away. Conagher could read women, even ten-year-olds, and from the look on her face, Joey had some strong feelings for Parmalee.

Parmalee approached the fire, and Conagher said, "I think there's a cup left in the pot."

"I'll get it," Parmalee said, and poured it himself.

"Still hold hard feelings, Parmalee?" Conagher asked.

"Yes."

"Against me, or against Mary?"

Parmalee didn't answer. Three years ago he'd made a terrible mistake. He had allowed himself to open up to a woman and feel, for the first time in years—and then Conagher had come along, and that was that.

"I want you to understand something, Lyle," Parmalee said.

"What's that?"

Parmalee looked to see where Laura was, and was satisfied that she was out of earshot. "The woman is off limits."

Conagher smiled and asked, "To me, or to you?"

"To both of us."

"You tryin' to tell me that you haven't had her yet, Parmalee?"

"Just listen to what I'm saying."

"But Parmalee," Conagher said, "the lady has already offered."

"Say no."

"Did you?"

Parmalee dumped the rest of his coffee into the

fire, which hissed and consumed it. He stared hard across the fire at Conagher.

"Remember what I said, Lyle," he warned. "She's off limits."

"Maybe you're just interested in her for yourself, huh, Parmalee?" Conagher asked.

Parmalee stopped and turned. "It would be best for everyone concerned if you'd ride out in the morning, Lyle. It would especially be best for you."

"Is that a threat, Parmalee?"

Parmalee ignored the question and walked away. Joey would be needing help with his horse. As he turned to leave, he saw that Laura had been watching them, her arms folded across her breasts. He held her gaze for a split second, then turned away.

Laura had noticed Parmalee and Conagher talking and decided to keep her distance. She imagined, since she had offered herself to both men, that she might be one of the subjects they were discussing. Considering Parmalee's reaction to her repeated offers, he might even be warning Conagher off. It seemed to her that would normally be the duty of a husband. Hers, however, did not seem to be noticing much beyond his cows these days.

Watching the two men together, she knew that Conagher was the younger and more handsome of the two, but given her choice, she would have preferred Parmalee.

She didn't seem to be having too many choices lately, though.

CHAPTER THIRTY

It bothered Preston Walton that Parmalee had been able to avoid his shot so easily. That meant that Parmalee had seen him, when he thought that he was being so careful. Also, the man's timing had been uncanny. He had leaped to the side just in time. A split second later, and he would have had a bullet buried in his back. After that incident, Walton was only too happy to leave Parmalee to Harry the Hat Ross.

Felix Hankman wasn't so sure about this job anymore. What should have been easy was taking too long and becoming too damned hard. Hankman was no longer all that anxious to take on Dan Parmalee. The man may have been out of the business for a few years, but from what Walt had told him, Parmalee's timing wasn't off even a little.

If his timing was perfect now, what must he have been like years ago?

When he found out about it, Harry the Hat wasn't surprised that Preston Walton had missed Parmalee—or rather, that Parmalee had managed to avoid being shot by Walton. If not for the woman, Walton would probably be dead. That, Ross thought, was enough to keep Walton from trying something that stupid again.

What Walton and Hankman didn't realize was that Parmalee was a special breed of man. His skills wouldn't have eroded over the last few years. Just because he had kept low to the ground did not mean that he had been inactive. And inactivity, to a man like Parmalee, didn't mean the same as it did to normal men.

No, Ross knew about men like Parmalee, and he was more than prepared to face him—but at a time and place of his own choosing.

He knew the special kind of man Dan Parmalee was, because he was the same kind of man.

They were two of a kind.

In his youth, before going to work for Max Venable, Rex Cameron had plied many trades. One of them had been that of a tracker, and he still possessed some of those skills. If he was reading the signs right, his camp was less than half a day behind the herd—and the men who were following it. He was now convinced that something was very wrong. That was the only explanation there could be for the fact that he hadn't yet come across Hankman, Walton and Ross.

If that was true, then he was going to have to take care of Parmalee himself, whatever way he could.

* * *

Parmalee roused himself and looked around. From where he was, he could see Conagher's outfit. The moonlight was bright enough for him to see that Conagher was asleep, wrapped in his blanket.

He had warned Conagher off, but he doubted that would mean anything to the man. Conagher had a habit of doing what he wanted to do. The only way Parmalee might get him to leave was to get Ted to ask him. Unfortunately, that would mean telling Ted what his wife had done, that she had not only offered herself to Parmalee, but to Conagher as well. Parmalee didn't want to do that, and it didn't have anything to do with not wanting to hurt Ted Shea's feelings. To tell him that now would put even more of a strain on the remainder of the drive, and they didn't need that. They still had three killers to deal with, and if they were fighting among themselves, that would give the killers an edge.

Parmalee decided that he was just going to have to keep a close eye on Laura and Conagher. Maybe that would convince Conagher to eventually leave. Laura was a lovely woman, and he couldn't blame Conagher for wanting her. He would want her for himself under different circumstances.

The fact was—and he hadn't admitted this to himself until now—that Laura reminded him a little of Mary Carter, the woman Conagher had taken from him in San Francisco three years ago. Already a bitter and cynical man at that point in his life, the experience with Mary and Conagher had served to make him even more so.

He certainly didn't want to go through that again. Laura was married to Ted, and Parmalee was going to do everything he could to keep Laura and Conagher apart—and to keep Ted from knowing what was going on while he was doing it.

He stood up, saddled his horse and rode out to relieve Ted.

Ted Shea looked out over his herd and tried to keep his mind both blank and alert. If he allowed himself to think about Laura, it might affect his alertness. He certainly had to deal with Laura, but he couldn't afford to give it any thought until this drive was over. Did she think he was a fool? That he couldn't see the way she looked at Parmalee? And now at Conagher, as well? It had been a long time since Ted and Laura had lain together as husband and wife, but Ted always had hope that they would find the love they'd had once again—if only he could get this herd delivered, keep the ranch, and fight off the long arms of Max Venable. He knew that Max wanted not only his daughter, Laura, but also his grand-daughter, Joey. Ted had admitted to himself a long time ago that even if Max *got* Laura, he would never let the old man have Joey—never! No matter what he had to do, that old man would not get his hands on Ted Shea's daughter.

Ted had even more respect for Parmalee for fending off Laura's advances, but he didn't have quite that much confidence in Conagher. The gambler was a good-looking man, and it was probably dangerous to have him in camp; but with three killers out there after them, it could only help to have another gun in camp. An extra gun meant that Joey was that much safer, as was the herd.

Ted was going to have to rely on Parmalee to watch Conagher. If the time came when it was more dangerous to have Conagher in camp than not, Parmalee would let him know. Aside from the fact that Parmalee had not mentioned Laura's advances—and Ted *knew* that there had been some—the man had been honest with him right from the beginning.

He had to rely now not only on Parmalee's abilities, but on his honesty as well.

Joey was confused.

Something was going on in camp that she was unable to understand. Her mother and father didn't talk all that much anymore, and earlier she had seen her mother talking with the new man, Conagher. She didn't like Lyle Conagher, and wished that either her father or Parmalee would ask him to leave camp.

She woke up in time to see Parmalee ride out to relieve her father, but had fallen back asleep by the time Ted Shea rode back into camp.

"You don't think we should have Conagher in camp," Ted said when Parmalee came out to relieve him. "I mean, now that I know you're not objecting just because he's a stranger."

"Conagher's character is suspect," Parmalee said.

"You think he might be working for the others?" Ted asked.

"No," Parmalee said, "that's not what I mean." At that point he almost told Ted about Laura, but decided against it. "What I mean is that he's a disruptive influence—he's been disruptive anywhere he's gone. He actually *likes* to start trouble."

"He didn't start it yesterday, in Kenicut."

"No," Parmalee said with a frown, "he didn't, I admit that."

"We could use the extra gun, Parmalee."

Parmalee looked at Ted and said, "You can always use an extra gun, Ted, and Conagher can use his. I've seen him."

"Then we'll have him stay with us," Ted said, "for a while?"

After a moment's hesitation, Parmalee nodded and repeated, "For a while."

Lyle Conagher saw Parmalee saddle up and ride out to relieve Ted Shea. He looked over at the wagon, where Joey Shea was sleeping underneath and Laura Shea inside. It was too dangerous to try anything now. He turned onto his back, laced his hands together behind his head and stared at the sky. The situation in camp was volatile. Laura Shea's attitude made it so, and Parmalee's presence made it even more so. He remembered with fondness the look on Parmalee's face when he found out that Mary Carter was sleeping with Conagher. Here he had two men to worry about—Shea and Parmalee—and that only made the situation that much more appealing to him.

Once again Lyle Conagher was playing with fire, and he felt very much alive.

CHAPTER THIRTY-ONE

DAY FORTY-SIX: "Conagher's been with us three days now, and despite Parmalee's misgivings and my own, the man has given us three days of good work. He's taking a watch at night, and having a third man helping to drive the herd has increased our progress. We've done a consistent twelve miles each of the past three days.

"This may work out."

DAY FIFTY: "Conagher is still pulling his weight, but if I'm noticing the looks between him and Laura at the campfire in the evenings, what about Parmalee? And what about Joey? She's become very quiet of late, and I think she senses that something is wrong between her mother and me.

"The poor kid must be confused."

"I'm confused."
Parmalee looked down at Joey, who was seated

next to him. Laura was cleaning up after dinner, and both Ted and Conagher had ridden out to check the herd. One of them would remain on watch, and the other would return.

Joey's statement came out like a confession, and that made Parmalee uncomfortable.

Still, he asked, "About what?"

"My mother and father," she said.

"What about them?"

She shrugged, looked down at the ground and said, "They don't seem to like each other anymore."

"Well, Joey—"

She looked up at him and said, "Please don't tell me I'm magining things. That's what grownups always tell kids, that they're imagining things."

"Well, I wasn't going to tell you that," Parmalee said.

"Then you notice it, too?"

"Joey," Parmalee said, "sometimes, when people have to live through hardships, like your mother and father are doing now, it drives them apart."

"For always?" Joey asked. "Or only until the hardships are over?"

"Well . . . that depends."

"On what?"

"On how much they really love each other, I guess."

"Do you think my mother and father really love each other?"

"Honey," Parmalee said, "you would probably know that better than I would."

"Well, they loved each other before I came along, I guess," she said, studying the problem. "And after I came, they loved each other. Lately, though—even before we started this drive—they argued a lot."

"People in love argue, Joey," Parmalee explained. "Even if you love someone, that doesn't mean you get along with them all the time."

"What about you?"

"What about me?"

"Have you been in love?"

Parmalee hesitated, then said, "Once or twice."

"Didn't you ever love a woman enough to want to marry her?"

"No."

"Why not?"

"You're getting nosy, Joey."

"I love you, Parmalee," Joey said. "Did you know that?"

Parmalee cleared his throat. "Uh, no, I didn't."

"Well, I've told you," she said. "I told myself I wouldn't, but I have . . . and it doesn't matter if you don't love me back. That's okay."

"Joey—"

"My mother said she didn't think you were . . . capable of loving someone."

"She said that?"

"Yes," Joey said, staring at him with wide, liquid eyes, "but I don't believe that for a minute." She stood up abruptly and kissed Parmalee on the cheek. "I'm gonna go and help Ma."

She ran off, and Parmalee touched the spot on his cheek where she had kissed him.

Joey still made Parmalee uncomfortable, but

for a different reason. Before, it was because he didn't like kids, didn't know how to act around them. He still didn't quite know how to act around her, but more and more lately he found himself looking forward to seeing her, and talking to her. She was so painfully honest, so fresh and unjaded that it was a pleasure to be in her company.

She was the only honest person in camp. Laura certainly wasn't being honest with Ted. Conagher was dishonest at heart. Parmalee didn't think that Ted was being honest with himself. And Parmalee himself? He wasn't being honest with Ted about Laura, he wasn't being honest with Joey about her parents, and he wasn't even honest with Conagher about Mary. He still held that against Conagher. He had to admit that if he was going to be honest with himself.

Now he had to be honest with himself about the little girl. Parmalee never would have thought that he could be loved by a little girl, or that he could love her, but apparently both were true.

He admitted to himself that he loved the little girl. Now he just had to get to the point where he stopped thinking of that as a weakness.

Conagher was the one who returned from the herd, which meant that Ted was taking the first watch. They had been alternating the watch so that no one ended up with the first each night, or the last.

"You can get some sleep," Conagher said when he returned. "I'll take the second watch."

Parmalee looked over at Laura and saw that she was watching them.

"Don't worry," Conagher said. "I don't think anything's going to happen tonight."

Parmalee didn't respond.

"It will happen, though, Parmalee," Conagher added. "Bet on it."

"You're the gambler, Conagher," Parmalee said. "Just don't make the stakes too high."

Conagher smiled at Parmalee. "The stakes can never get high enough to suit me, Parmalee."

Like most gamblers, Parmalee thought, Conagher thought he could never lose.

Like most gamblers, he was going to find out the hard way just how wrong he was.

"I've got an idea," Rex Cameron said.

The Venable foreman had caught up with Walton, Hankman and Ross two days ago, and had been riding with them ever since. After two days he was edgy, and didn't know how the other men could have waited as long as they had.

He had spoken to Walton in private, telling him how disappointed Max Venable was with them.

"This isn't easy, you know," Walton said. "The timing has to be right."

"It's been almost two months."

"And we tried twice. Once we almost lost Hank, and the other time they almost got me. Look, Rex, Harry's the only one who has a chance against Parmalee. We've got to leave the time and place to him."

"All right," Rex had said, "for now," but now he was just too edgy to wait.

And so. . . .

"What's the idea?" Harry the Hat asked.

"A stampede," Rex said.

The others exchanged glances.

"Don't tell me you fellas never even thought of it?" Rex asked.

"We're not cattlemen," Hankman said.

"During a stampede they'd be so damned busy that we'd be able to ride down and take care of Parmalee," Rex explained, then added, "that is, if the cows don't take care of him for us."

After a moment, Harry said, "I don't like it."

"He just wants to face Parmalee down," Hankman said.

"What about you, Walt?" Rex asked.

"Sounds good to me."

"Hankman?"

"I vote yes."

They all looked at Harry the Hat, and he returned their looks frankly.

"I'll go along," he said, "only because I don't think it'll work."

"Why not?" Rex asked.

"Parmalee's too good to go down that way."

"Nobody's as good as you think Parmalee is," Cameron said, and then added to himself, *or as good as you think you are.*

"We'll see," Harry said.

CHAPTER THIRTY-TWO

They waited until well after dark, and then rode down toward the herd. Since Cameron was with them, they at least had an experienced cowman to follow. Left to their own devices, the three gunmen would never have gotten anywhere near the herd without spooking the cows and alerting whoever was on watch.

Cameron kept them downwind from the herd so that the cows wouldn't smell them or the horses they were riding. He gave the other three their instructions in camp, going over it time and again, so that they wouldn't have to speak at all after leaving camp.

The four men knew exactly what they had to do to stampede Ted Shea's herd.

One thing that Rex Cameron had made very clear before leaving was the direction the herd was to be stampeded.

"Under no circumstances," he said, "are these

cows to be sent runnin' through their camp. Got that? That would be putting Mr. Venable's daughter and granddaughter in danger, and we don't want that, do we?" He felt as if he were talking to three children.

"We understand that," Walton said.

"Yeah," Hankman said.

Ross didn't comment, but he nodded so that the foreman would know he understood.

"Then let's get it done."

Ted Shea was about fifteen minutes away from being relieved by Conagher when he realized that something was wrong. He didn't know exactly what it was, but it was a feeling he had that he wasn't alone. He stood in his stirrups and looked out over the herd. They were standing quietly. If something was wrong, surely they'd sense it and react.

That was, if trouble wasn't downwind. Ted looked downwind, and the moonlight helped him to see the silhouettes of the mounted men; but he was too late. Once the first shot was fired, the cows were spooked, and when the other shots followed, they were off and running.

All Ted had to hope was that he could keep them from running through camp.

Cameron led the way down to the herd, two men on one side, and two men on the other. The gunmen had orders not to fire until he did, and then to fire only in the air. Cameron didn't know what happened, but someone fired too soon, and the cows were off—in the wrong direction.

* * *

Hankman saw Ted Shea look over toward him, and instinctively he raised his gun and fired at the man. He missed, cursed himself, and then realized what he had done. Quickly he holstered his weapon, hoping that the others wouldn't notice who fired first.

Parmalee heard the shots and came awake immediately. On the heels of the shots he heard the rumble of the cows' hooves on the ground.

He looked up and saw Conagher, who was frozen in motion. He had probably been on his way to relieve Ted Shea. His head was cocked as he listened, and when he realized what was happening, he looked toward Parmalee.

"Stampede!" Parmalee shouted.

He couldn't really tell if the cows were heading their way, but he couldn't afford to take the chance.

"Conagher, get on your horse," he shouted, coming to his feet. "If they're headed this way, we'll have to try and turn them."

"We can't—"

"It's a small herd," Parmalee said, brushing away the man's protest. "We might be able to do it."

Parmalee ran to the wagon as Joey was scrambling out from beneath it. She slept dressed, as did Laura, who dropped down from the wagon.

"What happened?" Laura demanded.

"Stampede!"

"How?"

"I don't know," Parmalee said. "It doesn't matter. Get mounted."

"We should stay in the wagon."

"Get mounted!" he shouted again. "You'll have a better chance on horseback."

Laura picked a good time to decide not to argue with him. "Joey, get your saddle—"

"No saddle," Parmalee interrupted. "There's no time. Ride bareback, and hang on. If they get through, ride with them."

"But—"

"Come on, Mommy," Joey said, tugging at her mother's hand.

Parmalee ran to his horse and mounted bareback. Conagher, who had been preparing to relieve Ted, had already saddled his horse.

As Parmalee rode up to him, he turned and said, "They're headed this way."

"Well," Parmalee said, "get out your gun and let's try to turn 'em."

Ted knew that trying to turn the stampeding herd was no use. Getting into camp ahead of them was out of the question, too. All he could do was worry about Laura and Joey, and try to stay alive himself.

"Fire!" Parmalee shouted. "Ride right at them and fire!"

Parmalee kicked his horse in the ribs and, mane in one hand and gun in the other, rode toward the oncoming herd.

"Shit," Conagher said, "he's crazy."

Conagher didn't mind firing his gun, but he'd be damned if he was going to ride right into the teeth of a stampeding herd.

"Look, Mommy," Joey said from astride her horse. "Parmalee's ridin' right into the herd."

"He's crazy," Laura mumbled, half to herself.

"Ma," Joey said, her eyes filled with panic, "where's Pa?"

Parmalee emptied his gun, and when it became obvious that there was no stopping the herd, that they were going to run right through camp, he holstered his gun, turned his horse and started the other way.

"That's it!" Cameron shouted to the others. "Nothin's gonna stop them now."

The others gathered around him, and they watched the herd thunder its way toward the camp.

"It's goin' right through the camp," Harry the Hat said.

Cameron's eyes widened as he realized that Ross was right. The herd was going to go right through the camp, where Laura and Joey Shea were.

Parmalee could see Laura and Joey riding ahead of him, but he didn't know where Conagher was— and he had no idea at all where Ted Shea was.

"Shit!" Cameron shouted.

"You didn't notice?" Ross asked.

Cameron looked at the three of them in turn and asked, "Who fired the first shot?"

Watson said, "I thought you did."

"I didn't fire until I heard a shot," Ross said.

Hankman—a terrible liar all his life—hesitated just long enough to give himself away. When he did speak, it came out very defensively.

"Not me!"

"Damn it, Hankman!" Cameron cursed.

Before Cameron could go any further, Ross said, "Can we go somewhere else and fight about this?"

Cameron clenched his jaw, then said, "You're right. Let's get out of here."

Cameron turned his horse and rode away from the herd. He just hoped the little girl and her mother would come out of this okay. If they didn't, he wouldn't be looking only for a new job, but a new life and someplace to live it where Max Venable wouldn't find him.

CHAPTER THIRTY-THREE

The only sound that Parmalee could hear was the pounding of the herd's hooves, filling the air just like thunder. That was probably where the phrase "thundering hooves" came from, he figured inanely. Fine time to be identifying and defining terms.

Ahead of him, he watched Laura and Joey ride bareback. Joey seemed to be having no problem, but Laura was sitting the horse very unsurely. She kept sliding from side to side, grasping the horse's mane to try and steady herself. If she fell . . . He preferred not to think about that.

And then the unthinkable happened.

He watched as Laura started to slide to the right, as if in slow motion. He waited for her to correct the slide by leaning the other way, but she didn't—or couldn't. She kept moving to the right, farther and farther, until she looked almost comical, trying to hold on to the horse's neck, and then finally falling off.

As she hit the ground, Joey looked over and saw her fall.

"Mama!" she shouted.

Joey reined her horse in and started to turn it. Parmalee rode up alongside her and said, "I'll get her. Keep riding!" For extra emphasis, he slapped her horse on the rump.

As Joey started riding again, he turned and reached his hand down to Laura.

"Come on!" he yelled, but she wasn't looking at him. She was looking behind them, at the approaching herd, her eyes wide with fright.

"Laura, grab my hand!" he shouted, but it was as if she were mesmerized by what she saw. "Laura, you bitch, do what I tell you for once. Grab on!"

Finally, she tore her eyes away from the herd and reached up. Parmalee grabbed her forearm and pulled her up behind him on the horse.

"Hold on."

She wrapped her arms around his waist and held on tightly.

Having to stop for Laura cost Parmalee any lead he'd had on the herd. Suddenly, they were in the midst of the stampede, and the only thing keeping them from being trampled was their horse and its ability to run with the herd without becoming panicked. If the horse took a bad step, they'd be killed for sure.

* * *

Ted Shea was riding on the outside of the herd, keeping pace with it. They had already run through the camp, and he watched carefully as the wagon was overturned. He didn't think that Joey or Laura were in the wagon, and fervently hoped that he was right.

He hadn't seen any sign of his wife and daughter, or of Conagher and Parmalee. The herd was running back in the direction they had come from and would run until they were exhausted. He hoped that they wouldn't scatter as well, because then they'd have to hunt them down *and* give them time to rest. That, coupled with the fact that they might go for miles before stopping, undoing hours, maybe a day of their traveling, would put them even farther behind schedule than they were before.

There was nothing else he could do, though. Alone, he had no chance of stopping them, or even turning them. They would run until they could run no more, or maybe until they came to water.

He recalled with dismay that the last water they had passed was a small stream, nearly half a day's ride behind them.

Cameron, Harry the Hat and the others rode up onto a rise so that they could look down and see what kind of damage they had done.

"Jesus," Cameron said. He was looking at what was left of the Shea camp. The wagon had been overturned, the fire trampled out, and there was debris everywhere, stamped flat. Whatever horses hadn't been ridden had been spooked.

"I'm goin' down," Cameron said. "Wait here."

"For what?" Walton asked.

"I have to check and see if either Laura or Joey is down there."

"If they are, they're in the wagon," Ross said.

"I'll have a look," Cameron said. He looked at them and said again, "Wait here."

"That's fine with me," Hankman said. "I don't want to be down there in case the herd turns."

"That herd ain't turnin'," Ross said. "They won't stop runnin' for a long time."

Cameron thought the same thing, but his main worry now was if any harm had come to Laura or Joey.

Joey's heart was in her throat. She was still ahead of the herd, but she was worried about her mother and father, and about Parmalee. She looked back and saw Parmalee, still astride his horse, but right in the middle of the charging herd. Behind him, holding tightly to him, was her mother. If they should fall. . . .

She turned away and looked ahead of her. She was smart enough to know that if her horse took a bad step, she'd be in serious trouble. She had to keep her eyes cast forward, to try and make sure that didn't happen.

Cameron rode down into the camp, dismounted and hurried to the overturned wagon. A quick look inside satisfied him that neither Laura nor Joey was inside. He felt relieved, both for Laura and for himself. There was still a chance that no harm had come to them, and stampeding the herd would probably keep Ted Shea from getting his beeves to the railhead in time to sell them at a fair price. Even if he managed to get them there, he'd have to sell them at such a reduced price that he'd lose his ranch.

All that was left now was to make sure Parmalee was dead.

Laura held tightly to Parmalee, pressing herself up against him. She had been terrified up until the time he lifted her up onto his horse. Now, holding fast to him, she felt no fear.

If Ted could ever make her feel this way, maybe her marriage wouldn't be crumbling.

Cameron rode back up to where the others were waiting for him.

"So?" Walton asked.

"They're not down there," Cameron said, "either of them."

"Then where are they?" Hankman asked.

"On the run, I guess," Cameron said, "tryin' to outrun the herd."

"What about the others?" Ross asked. "What about Parmalee?"

"What about him?" Hankman said. "He's probably been trampled to death by now."

"We can't assume that," Ross said. "We've got to go and find him—either him or his body."

"Harry's right," Cameron said. "We've got to make sure he's dead."

Walton and Hankman exchanged glances, and then Walton said, "You know, I think we should be gettin' paid more for this."

"If we find Parmalee, and I kill him," Ross said, "you fellas can split my share."

Hankman laughed and said, "You don't want the money?"

"Once I kill Parmalee," Harry the Hat Ross said, "I won't need Max Venable's money."

Parmalee couldn't detect any sign of the herd's slowing down. If they caught the scent of water, they'd keep running until they reached it. Like Ted Shea, Parmalee remembered the stream they had passed half a day ago.

He hoped that his horse, and Joey's, could keep running that long.

CHAPTER THIRTY-FOUR

Parmalee's horse almost stumbled, but retained its feet. The animal was starting to weary, and it was time to try to work his way out from the midst of the herd.

Parmalee was satisfied to see that Joey was able to work her way outside of the herd and was now riding along with them from safety. The herd was starting to stretch out as some of the steers were tiring and others were still full of run. Parmalee and Laura were not as hemmed in as they had been earlier, and with his horse tiring, it was time to try to get to the outside.

It took some time, but Parmalee was gradually able to work his way to the edge of the herd, and then finally to the outside, on the same side as Joey. Once that was done, he reined in and signaled for Joey to do the same.

As Joey rode back to meet them, Parmalee lowered Laura to the ground. Joey dropped down from her horse and ran into her mother's arms.

Laura looked up at Parmalee over her daughter's head and said, "I don't know how to thank you. You saved my life back there."

"I didn't have any choice," he said. He looked behind them and saw a rider approaching. It took a few moments for him to get close enough to be identified.

"Here comes Ted."

"Daddy!" Joey shouted.

Ted dismounted and ran to his wife and daughter.

Laura was surprised at how glad she was to see Ted. When he took her and Joey into his arms, Laura actually felt tears come to her eyes. Maybe she wasn't so out of love with her husband as she thought.

Ted looked at Parmalee and said, "Thank you for savin' my family."

"Now we've got to do something about saving your herd," Parmalee said.

"I don't know if it's even worth it," Ted said. "Even if we get them to Kansas Railhead in Ellsworth, it'll be too late. I'll have to sell them for ten cents on the dollar."

"So?" Parmalee said. "Maybe that won't save your ranch, but it'll give you a stake to start over again."

"Start over?" Ted asked. "Where?"

"Anywhere but where we just came from," Parmalee said. "Away from Max Venable."

"He's still Laura's father," Ted said.

"This is something for you and your family to talk over," Parmalee said, "but later. Right now we've got to trail that herd and see where they end up."

"Water, probably."

"That's what I figure," Parmalee said. "I hate to do this, Laura, but you and Joey are going to have to ride back to camp and salvage whatever you can. Ted and I have to try and round up the herd."

"What happened to Conagher?" Ted asked.

"I don't know," Parmalee said, "but I can guess. He was with me when the stampede started, and I guess he lit out."

"Can't say that I blame him," Ted said. "This was probably much more than he bargained for."

"I can blame him," Parmalee said. "Ted, what started the stampede?"

"Riders," Ted explained, "three or four of them. They rode down on the herd and started firing before I had a chance to do anything."

"Wasn't much you could have done about it, anyway," Parmalee assured him. "I'd say the riders aren't strangers to us."

"The men Max hired," Ted said, and Parmalee nodded.

"Laura, you and Joey will share her horse. If you see any of the other horses, try to retrieve them. If you can't, then don't worry about it. The most important thing is to see what you can salvage from camp, specifically any food or water."

"We understand," Laura said, putting her arm around Joey's shoulder.

"Here," Parmalee said. He took an old Colt

from his saddlebag and handed it to Laura. "It doesn't look like much, but I keep it in firing condition."

She took it from him.

"Can you handle it?"

"I can handle it," she said. She patted Joey on the shoulder and said, "Let's go, Joey."

"Start back this way with whatever you find," Parmalee said. "We'll be bringing the herd back and meet you along the way."

"All right."

Ted walked with Joey and Laura to Joey's horse and boosted both of them up. He had wanted to give them his saddled horse, but Parmalee told him that they would need the saddled horses to work the herd.

Laura and Joey waved and started riding back toward the camp.

"What if they run into those men?" Ted asked.

"If my guess is right," Parmalee said, "they have instructions not to harm Laura or Joey."

"That makes sense," Ted said, "since they work for Max, but what about the stampede?"

"Guessing again," Parmalee said, "I'd say the herd got out of control. I don't think they deliberately stampeded them through camp."

"Well, whether it was deliberate or not," Ted said, "it just about finished us."

"Forget that talk, Ted," Parmalee said. "Let's go and find those beeves, huh?"

"All right, Parmalee."

Parmalee looked around while Ted mounted up. He didn't think they were being watched, and he didn't see any sign of Conagher. That was just as well. If he saw the gambler again, he might just kill him.

"They're too far from home to start back," Cameron said.

He had decided not to chase down the herd and see who had survived. They had essentially achieved what Max Venable had been after, and that was to keep Ted Shea from getting his herd to Kansas in time to sell at full price.

"What are you sayin'?" Ross asked.

"Whatever shape they're in," Cameron said, "they'll continue on to Ellsworth, and we'll be there waiting for them. I'll be able to send Mr. Venable a telegraph message from there."

"And I can wait for Parmalee to come ridin' in," Ross said.

"If he's alive," Hankman added.

"He's alive," Ross said. "I can feel it."

They had ridden the trail of the stampeded herd for a couple of hours, and had not come upon any bodies. That seemed to be enough to convince Harry the Hat that Parmalee was still alive.

"You really think you can take Parmalee, don't you?" Hankman asked.

"I know I can," Harry the Hat said. With two fingers he sort of caressed the brim of his white hat.

"So, we'll ride on to Ellsworth then, and wait," Cameron decided.

"Fine with me," Hankman said. "I've had enough trail dust to last me forever. The next job I take is gonna be in a real town, like Frisco."

"Do we get paid when we get to Ellsworth?" Walton asked.

"You get paid when I say the job's done, Preston," Cameron said. "I hope you—any of you—don't have a problem with that."

"As long as we get paid," Preston Walton said, "I got no problems at all."

CHAPTER THIRTY-FIVE

DAY—"What does it matter what day it is? I am totally demoralized. My father-in-law's men have succeeded in stampeding the herd, driving us back a half a day in distance and time, and more. We shall have to round up the herd again and give them time to rest. We'll be very late getting to Ellsworth, Kansas, and I will have to sell my cattle for ten cents on the dollar.

"We have no chuck wagon, very few supplies, so we are forced to ration food. Water is plentiful, because the herd ran all the way back to the stream we passed earlier.

"Parmalee says we should continue on, but that is easy for him to say. When we are finished, he will go his way, go on with his life. What kind of life will we have, Joey, Laura, and I? Will I even have my daughter and my wife after this? Or will Laura go back to her father after all these years?

"Does it really matter anymore?"

* * *

DAY . . . SIXTY-SOMETHING: "We have rounded up one hundred and ten head, with eighty or so still scattered. We recovered one extra horse. I am ready to drive the cattle we have to Ellsworth, but Parmalee wants to round up the rest. I am somewhat surprised at Laura's eagerness to go along with Parmalee. She and Joey are both working hard, rounding up strays. Am I the only one who has given up?"

Parmalee drank his coffee and looked across the camp at Ted Shea. Of late, Ted's carriage had taken on an uncharacteristic shoulder slump. The man seemed to have totally given up. On the other hand, Laura Shea was burning with a new fire. She seemed incensed that her father would send men to stampede a herd of cattle through their camp, endangering not only her, but Joey, his own granddaughter.

"I don't care if we only get one animal to Ellsworth," she said to Parmalee. "I'll sell that one animal and show the money to my father."

Joey seemed to react to the fire that burned within her mother, and was working like a demon.

Parmalee was even surprised at himself. He was the one who initially insisted that they continue to round up cattle until they had as many back as they could get. Now he, Laura and Joey were working with vigor while Ted Shea seemed only to be going through the motions.

Laura came up alongside Parmalee now and poured some more coffee into his cup, then looked over at her husband.

"I've never seen him like this."

"The stampede really seems to have taken a lot out of him," Parmalee observed.

"It's funny," she said, shaking her head.

"What is?"

"I'm so angry with my father I can't think about anything but getting this herd to Ellsworth. I think I know what Ted's been feeling all this time."

Parmalee looked at Laura, reached over and took the coffeepot from her. "Why don't you tell him that?"

"I—I wouldn't know what to say."

"Just say what you're feeling," Parmalee said. "I think it would do him a lot of good."

Laura gave Parmalee a worried look and then started walking toward Ted.

Joey came over to Parmalee and said, "What's goin' on, Parmalee?"

"Your mother and father are going to talk," Parmalee said.

Joey smiled.

After talking with Laura for a while, Ted Shea wandered over to the fire, where Parmalee was finishing his coffee. In a moment Parmalee would go out and keep watch over the herd, even though he doubted that Venable's men were still around. They had accomplished what they were supposed to.

"Any left?" Ted asked, grabbing a cup.

"Some."

Ted picked up the pot and poured what was left into his cup, grains and all. Parmalee had noticed that about Ted earlier on in the drive. He usually drank the last cup out of the pot, and then chewed the grains.

"I had a talk with Laura," Ted said.

"Good."

"Actually, she did most of the talking."

Parmalee remained silent.

"She says we should deliver the cattle to Ellsworth just to spite her father."

"Sounds good to me."

"There would be a certain amount of satisfaction in that, I admit," Ted said, "but—"

"But what?"

"It's not for very much more than that, is it?"

Parmalee shrugged. "That's for you to decide, Ted," he said. "I'm not going to push you."

"You've been pushing me, Parmalee," Ted said, "and I thank you for it; but you won't have to push me anymore. We'll get these animals delivered, pay you what you've got coming, and see what we can do with what we have left."

"I'll be with you right to the end," Parmalee said. "I've got to get out to the herd."

"I'll relieve you in three hours."

"All right."

Parmalee mounted his horse and rode out to where the herd stood. For the most part, the longhorns were still standing with their heads down, suffering from the effects of their long run.

Parmalee sat his horse with ease, for he knew what was waiting for him in Ellsworth. That would be when he got *his* satisfaction. Somehow, he knew that Venable's men—maybe his foreman, and the three men who had been dogging their trail for the entire drive—would be there. Venable would want his man there just to make sure he knew when Ted Shea finally arrived. Cameron would probably send the old man a telegram when Parmalee, Ted and the others rode into Ellsworth.

Parmalee, on the other hand, had his own special delivery to send. There were three men, maybe four, to whom he owed a debt, and he was a man who always paid off.

What surprised Parmalee—and he was surprising himself quite a bit lately—was that he felt no personal animosity toward the men. That is, he was not going to pay them back for putting *him* in danger, but for putting Joey in danger. He had not realized how close he had become to that little girl until that herd went charging through the camp. The whole time he was riding in the midst of the stampeding herd, even with Laura clinging tightly to him, his eyes had been on Joey.

He wasn't used to having these feelings for someone else. He hadn't felt this way since Mary . . . and he didn't particularly like it. Still, there was nothing he could do about it.

Thinking about Mary made him think about Conagher. He had a debt to pay to the gambler, too, and this one *was* personal. The gambler had lit out at the start of the stampede, and was probably still running. If Parmalee ever crossed paths with Conagher again, the other man was not going to get another chance to walk—or run—away.

He guided his horse around the herd slowly. With all the debts he was piling up, and all the emotions he was having to deal with, he couldn't wait until this was all over with.

Ted Shea sat at the fire, munching coffee grains. From where he sat, he could see Laura and Joey bedding down together. Ever since the stampede, mother and daughter seemed to have gotten much closer, and Ted was very happy with that. He was also happy to see how hard Laura was working for the first time during the drive. He hadn't seen Laura this determined in a long time.

She had come up to him earlier to tell him how she was behind him all the way, and that they had to show her father that he couldn't beat them. Frankly, Ted wished she had felt like that at the start of the drive. He still felt that her feelings were too little, too late, but he also didn't want to be too harsh on her. At least she had come around to his way of thinking. Whether or not they could make their marriage work after this was all over still remained to be seen.

Laura lay down next to Joey and once again thanked God that the child had not been hurt during the stampede. She knew that for the past few years she had not been a very good mother. She now felt that by keeping Joey safe God had given her another chance, and she intended to make the most of it. She didn't know if she still had it in her to be a good wife to Ted, but she was going to be the best mother she could be to Joey.

CHAPTER THIRTY-SIX

DAY EIGHTY-SEVEN: "As unbelievable as it is, we are about two days' ride from Ellsworth. I use the word unbelievable. Do I mean that it is so unbelievable that we even made it? Or that we made it with about one hundred and forty head? Or how about unbelievable that we stuck with it through everything nature and Max Venable could throw our way?

"When we started, I didn't think Parmalee would last a week, and now it is he who pushed us to go all the way. He is a remarkable man, one I can still believe once made his living with a gun, killing people. But who I can also believe has become very close to my daughter, Joey.

"What awaits us after Ellsworth I do not know, but I am no longer overcome by grief, by depression, or by apprehension. Now I am simply waiting to see what will happen. . . ."

* * *

In Ellsworth, Felix Hankman and Preston Walton were becoming *more* than impatient. They had been in town almost three weeks, waiting for Parmalee or Shea to show up so that they could get their money—but what if they didn't show up? What if they had been killed in the stampede? What if they had just decided not to come to Ellsworth?

"They'll come," Rex Cameron assured them.

"When?" Walton asked.

"They'll come," was all Cameron would say.

Now Hankman and Walton, sitting in the saloon, decided it was time to get paid.

"Where's Ross?" Walton asked Hankman.

"Forget Ross," Hankman said. "All he does is spend time in the whorehouse, or sitting out in front of it, waiting for Parmalee. He doesn't care whether he gets paid or not."

"Well, I do," Walton said. "Let's find Cameron and get our money."

There were two saloons in Ellsworth. The Lucky Nickel was the one Hankman and Walton had been spending their time in. On the other hand, Rex Cameron had been patronizing the Pretty Lady. True to its name, the women who worked the saloon were *very* pretty, and it had enough gambling to satisfy the most die-hard of gamblers.

Upon arrival in Ellsworth, almost three weeks ago, Cameron had immediately sent off a telegram to Max Venable. He told the old man that the Shea herd had been stopped. He did not mention the stampede. He did not want Venable to know that his daughter and granddaughter had been in jeopardy. The reply he received from Venable was that Cameron should wait until Shea arrived in Ellsworth, for as long as it took. The old man even sent him a bank draft to hire extra men if he needed them to handle Parmalee.

Cameron had hired extra men, but he had hired them to take care of Hankman and Walton if they became impatient about being paid. The truth of the matter was, Cameron had no intention of paying them. They had botched the job all the way, and wouldn't be getting one red cent of Venable money. As for Harry the Hat, he didn't care about money. He wanted to be the man who killed Parmalee, and Cameron was going to give him that chance. The six other men that he had hired—cheap labor with guns—were simply backup, and insurance.

His other instructions were quite clear. When the Sheas got to Ellsworth, Cameron was to make sure that Laura and Joey Shea came home.

Cameron sat in the Pretty Lady Saloon now, watching the pretty ladies work the floor and the suckers lose their money. He had two men stationed outside to let him know when any riders came into town. One of the men came inside now and approached his table.

"Mr. Cameron?"

"What is it?"

"Hankman and Walton are headed this way."

Cameron nodded and said, "Tell the others."

"Yes, sir."

That was the kind of help to have, he thought. "Yes, sir," and "No, sir." Nothing at all like the two men who had just entered the saloon and were approaching his table.

"Boys," he said.

"Never mind," Walton said. "It's time to settle up, Cameron."

"Is it?"

"Yeah, it is," Hankman said.

"I thought I was the one who said when it was time to settle up."

"Not anymore," Walton said, "We want our money."

"We want what's comin' to us," Hankman said.

Cameron smiled and leaned back in his chair. "Well, boys, I think you deserve to get what's comin' to you."

"Damn right we do," Walton said.

"Nothin'," Cameron stated.

Walton frowned, and Hankman said, "Say that again?"

"I said you're gettin' nothin'," Rex Cameron repeated. "That's what you got comin'."

"What the hell are you talkin' about?"

"You didn't do what you were bein' paid to do," Cameron said. "It's as simple as that."

"We made sure that herd didn't get here in time for Shea to sell it at full price. You said yourself his buyer is gone."

"That was me," Cameron said. "I'm the one who did that. You fellas had almost two months to get the job done, and you didn't. Why, Parmalee is even still alive."

"That was Ross," Hankman said. "He kept sayin' he wanted Parmalee for himself."

"That was your mistake," Cameron said to Walton. "You brought Ross into it; you should have dealt with him."

"This is a double cross," Walton said, "and I don't like it."

He started to go for his gun, and Cameron said, "I wouldn't do that, Preston."

"Why not?"

Cameron pointed over toward the bar. The saloon had grown quiet as everyone's attention was drawn to the confrontation between the three men—only it wasn't between *only* the three men. Walton and Hankman looked toward the bar and saw five men holding guns on them.

"What the hell is this?" Walton said. "We made a deal, Rex."

Cameron smiled as Walton used his first name, trying to be buddies.

"And you broke it," Cameron said. "Mr. Venable is very disappointed in the two of you. He said I should not only *not* pay you, but that I should have you killed."

"H-hey—" Hankman said nervously. "Wait a minute—"

"See these boys? I already paid them half their money, and they're more than willin' to earn the other half."

"What makes them think they're gonna get paid any more than we did?" Walton asked.

"They understand that to get paid, the job has to be done," Cameron explained. "Now, if you boys aren't out of here in one minute, I'm gonna lift my hand, and those fellas are gonna kill you."

Walton looked tense, as if he was going to draw his gun anyway, but Hankman put his hand on the other man's arm.

"Don't, Preston," he said. "The odds ain't in our favor here."

"And they never will be," Cameron said. "If I ever see either of you again, I'll kill you myself."

"Try it now," Walton invited, but Hankman increased the pressure on his arm and pulled him toward the door.

Cameron watched as the two men backed out of the saloon, then waved for one of the hired guns to come over.

"I don't want them in town come tomorrow mornin'," he said.

"What if they don't wanna leave?" the man asked.

Cameron gave the man a hard stare and said, "Convince them."

The man nodded and went back to the bar to relay the message to the others. As they left, Cameron motioned to one of the pretty ladies.

"How would you like to get me a beer, and sit and talk awhile?" he asked her, waving a five-dollar bill at her.

"It's yours, honey," the girl said, taking the bill and tucking it down her dress.

As she walked to the bar, Cameron marveled at the power money had over people.

Out on the street, Preston Walton said, "He can't get away with this. I didn't spend two months of my life eating trail dust for nothin'." He turned and stared belligerently at the saloon. "We should have called his bluff."

For once the voice of reason was Felix Hankman's, and not Walton's.

"Bluff? What could we do against five guns, Preston? Be reasonable."

"We got to do somethin'," Walton said. "We can't let them get away with a double cross."

As he was staring at the saloon, several of Cameron's new men stepped out on the boardwalk and stared back.

"Come on," Hankman said, once again tugging on Walton's arm.

They walked to the hotel and stopped out front.

"Wait a minute," Hankman said. "I just thought of something."

"What?"

"If he ain't payin' us, then that means he ain't payin' Ross, either. Right?"

"So? We both know Ross don't care about money," Walton said.

"Ross don't care about it because he don't want it," Hankman said. "What if he knew that Cameron never intended to pay him, anyway? Do you think he'd let Cameron and the old man get away with that?"

"I don't know," Walton said, looking as if he liked the idea. "Why don't we ask him?"

Walton and Hankman found Harry the Hat Ross right where they thought they would, seated on a straight-backed wooden chair in front of the whorehouse. He had the chair leaning back on the rear two legs, and his eyes beneath his big white hat appeared to be drooping. They knew, though, that Ross saw them coming.

"Ross."

"What can I do for you fellas?"

"We just come from talkin' with Cameron," Felix Hankman said.

"So?"

"We told him we wanted to get paid."

"So?" Ross said, again. "I told you fellas you could split my share."

"There ain't no share to split," Hankman said.

"What do you mean?"

"There ain't no money," Walton said. "Cameron said that Venable ain't payin' us."

Ross tipped the hat farther up on his head and looked at the two men.

"Didn't you say we had a deal?"

"That's right, we did," Walton said, "but Cameron ain't payin' us, and that's that."

They had decided not to tell Ross the reason Cameron had given. It would serve their purpose better if Ross thought he wasn't being paid just out of pure meanness.

"That isn't right," Ross said.

"Well, we know you don't care about the money," Walton said, "but we just thought you'd like to know that none of us is gettin' any."

"I don't care about the money," Ross said, "but this is different."

"Whataya mean?" Walton asked innocently.

"If I don't want the money, that's one thing," Ross said, "but if Cameron and Venable aren't abiding by the deal, that's something else. I mean, I've got the money comin' to me whether I want it or not."

"That sounds right," Hankman said.

"What do you suppose we should do about it?" Walton asked.

"Where is Cameron?"

"He's in the Pretty Lady," Hankman said, and as Ross started to rise, he added, "but he's got a half a dozen new guns to back him up."

Ross sat back down. "You boys up to doin' somethin' about this?" Ross asked.

"You name it," Walton said.

"Just let me think on it a spell," Ross said. "I'll come up with somethin'."

Now, Hankman and Walton didn't want that. Parmalee might come ridin' into town any time, and if he killed Harry the Hat Ross—instead of the other way around—they wouldn't have Ross's gun to back their play.

"Shouldn't we ought do somethin' right now?" Hankman asked.

"You can't just walk into six guns, Hank," Harry the Hat said, leaning his chair back against the wall again. "That isn't smart. Cameron's not goin' anywhere—leastwise, not until Shea or Parmalee comes into town. Just let me think it over and I'll come up with somethin'."

Hankman and Walton exchanged a glance, then Walton shrugged.

"We'll be around, Harry," Walton said. "Just let us know when you're ready."

"I'll let you know."

* * *

As Walton and Hankman walked away, Ross studied their retreating backs. The two men had their heads together and were obviously cooking something up between them. The first thing Ross was going to have to do was talk to Cameron, and make sure those two jackals were telling the truth. He'd wait until after he killed Parmalee, though.

He didn't want anything interfering with that.

CHAPTER THIRTY-SEVEN

FINAL DAY: "We're right outside Ellsworth now, and it's time for me to go in and find a buyer. Parmalee's riding with me, because he's sure that Rex Cameron will be there with some men— probably the men who were trailing us, and who stampeded the herd.

"It's odd, but I'm not sure what I want to do about the stampede. Certainly Max was behind it, and Cameron probably engineered it. What should I do? Kill Cameron? Kill Max? Leave it to Parmalee?

"Parmalee suggests that we simply ride into town and see what happens.

"I've decided that's just what we'll do."

"When we get to town," Parmalee said to Laura and Joey, "we'll try to hire some men to come out and sit the herd with you."

"How are we going to pay—" Laura started, but Parmalee stopped her.

"Don't worry about that. Just expect them, and don't blow their heads off."

"How will we know they're from you?" Joey asked.

Parmalee thought a moment, then said, "I'll have one of them give you a bullet. You'll know it's from me."

"Be careful," Laura said, "both of you. If Rex Cameron is there, who knows what will happen?"

"I know," Parmalee said. "I know what's going to happen."

Laura saw the cold look in Parmalee's eyes when he said that, and she inadvertently shivered.

When they were just a few hundred yards from town Parmalee stopped, and Ted stopped beside him.

"What is it?"

"I just want to get something clear," Parmalee said. "We ride into town nice and easy, like nothing's wrong. If you see Cameron, or anyone else you know, just ignore them, okay?"

"Like who else?"

"Like the men we saw in Dennison."

"Or like Conagher?"

"Yes," Parmalee said, "like Conagher. If we see any of these men, I'll take care of them. All you're going to do is sell your cattle."

"If there's gunplay," Ted said, "I'll back you up, Parmalee."

"If there's gunplay, Ted," Parmalee said, "just

get out of the way so that I don't have to worry about you."

"Mr. Cameron?"

"What is it?"

"Strangers ridin' in, sir."

"How many?"

"Two."

Rex Cameron got up from his table and walked to the batwing doors. He looked out without stepping out.

"That's them," Cameron said. "Tell the others to be ready."

The man nodded and stepped into the saloon as Cameron moved out. Cameron stepped down into the street and walked out to the center, into the path of Parmalee and Ted Shea.

"Looks like we won't have a chance to ignore him," Ted said.

"Let's go easy," Parmalee said. "Nothing has to happen right now."

"Hank!"

Hankman came out of the Lucky Nickel Saloon to join Walton, who was seated outside.

"What is it?"

"They're here," Walton said.

Hankman looked up the street and saw Parmalee and Ted Shea riding in.

"I don't see no cattle."

"They're not gonna bring the cattle into town until Shea has a buyer."

"What the hell is Cameron doin'?" Hankman asked.

"I don't know," Walton said, "but let's watch."

Parmalee and Ted Shea reined in their horses about ten feet from Cameron.

"You boys look like you've had a hard trip," Cameron said.

"You'd know more about that than we would," Parmalee said.

"How would I know that?"

"You're the one who started the stampede," Parmalee said.

"What stampede?"

"Why, the one that killed Mrs. Shea and little Joey."

Cameron opened his mouth to speak, shut it abruptly, and then said, "Wha-a-at?"

Ted Shea almost said, "What?" before he realized what Parmalee was doing. Thinking that he had caused the deaths of his boss's daughter and granddaughter would throw Rex Cameron into a state of confusion.

"You heard me, Cameron," Parmalee said. "That stampede you and your boys started crushed the life out of your boss's family."

"You're crazy," Cameron said. "I checked—"

"Checked what?" Parmalee asked when the foreman stopped short. "The camp? It didn't happen in camp. We managed to get out of camp, but the cattle took down their horses, and they went under."

"And you didn't save them? Mr. Venable's not gonna like that."

Parmalee leaned forward in his saddle and said, "Maybe we couldn't save them, Cameron, but it was you who killed them. How do you think your boss is going to feel about that?"

Again, Cameron opened his mouth to speak, but no words came.

"Step aside," Parmalee said, starting his horse forward. "We have funeral arrangements to make."

Cameron, thoroughly confused about what to do next, moved out of the way before Parmalee rode him down.

As they rode on, Ted Shea said, "That was brilliant."

"It'll give you time to get to the stockyards and do what you have to do," Parmalee said.

"What are you going to be doing?"

"Making sure no one interferes with you."

Riding farther down the street, Parmalee saw the two men from Dennison standing in front of the saloon. As he looked their way, they averted their eyes. On the other side of the street sat a man in a big, wide-brimmed, white hat. Parmalee knew the hat, and the man under it.

"Ross," he said.

"What?" Ted asked.

"Harry the Hat Ross."

"Where?"

"Don't turn your head."

"I've heard of him," Ted said. "Do you think Max hired him?"

"Max, or Cameron."

"He's supposed to be very good with a gun."

"I know."

"Parmalee—"

"Keep going to the stockyards, Ted," Parmalee said. "Hire a couple of men to go out and look after the herd, and then get your best price."

"But I should—"

"I'm going to see about rooms in the hotel for all of us," Parmalee said. "Joey and Laura will be looking forward to a good meal, and a soft bed for a change."

"Parmalee—"

"Just go and take care of your business," Parmalee said, "while I take care of mine."

"Jesus," Hankman said, "he's comin' this way."

"Stand your ground," Walton said. "He's just comin' to get a room."

"And maybe he's comin' to get us," Hankman said.

Walton licked his lips and dropped his hand down by his gun. "If he is," he said, "there ain't much we can do about it now."

Parmalee rode directly to the hotel, stopped his horse right in front of the two men and dismounted. He stared at them for a moment while they both fidgeted from foot to foot, then turned and walked across the street to where Harry the Hat Ross was sitting.

CHAPTER THIRTY-EIGHT

Parmalee walked right up to the man in the white hat and said, "I never could figure out why a man in your business would make a target out of himself by wearing that white hat."

From beneath the hat Ross said, "Vanity." He pushed the hat up from his eyes so that he could look at Parmalee. "Or maybe I'm just that good. Hello, Parmalee."

"Harry the Hat. Don't tell me you hired on for this?" Parmalee asked.

"In the beginning," Ross said, "I figured, everybody's got to do something to make money. Later, when I found out you were involved, I figured, who needs money?"

"You're not going to tell me you came along for the ride just for the pleasure of killing me."

"There won't be any pleasure involved, Parmalee," Ross said, "believe me."

"Then why do it?"

Ross spread his hands. "You're here; I'm here," he said. "Why not?"

"We're not kids anymore, Harry," Parmalee said, "This sort of thing is for kids."

"What sort of thing?"

"Killing a man to increase your own reputation."

"Is that what I'm doing?"

Parmalee shrugged. "That's what you think you're doing," he said. "Believe me, killing me is not going to do that much for you."

Ross smiled. "You're underestimating yourself."

"Not really."

Ross looked across the street. "You've got those two shook up."

Parmalee glanced over his shoulder, and then back at Ross. "Who are they?"

"Felix Hankman and Preston Walton."

"Ah," Parmalee said. "I've heard of Walton. He's a backshooter."

"The best."

"He took a shot at me and missed."

"Doesn't sound like him."

"I never heard of the other one."

"He's not much."

"What about the foreman?"

"Well, I hear he hired about five or six guns here in town, and he's refusing to pay us what he owes us. He figures we didn't get the job done quick enough, I guess."

"What do you plan on doing about that?"

"Well," Ross said, "whatever I'm planning comes after you and I settle up."

"You were in on that stampede, weren't you?"

Ross nodded. "Not in favor of it, but in on it, yeah. It was the foreman's idea."

"Yeah, well, I think he's having second thoughts about it."

"When do you want to do this?" Ross asked.

Parmalee stared at the man and said, "You really plan on going through with it?"

"I don't feel like I have much of a choice."

"Well, I'm feeling a little played out at the moment. You wouldn't want people to say I wasn't at my best, would you?"

"No problem," Ross said. "I'll be here when you're rested enough."

"Maybe, while you're waiting," Parmalee said, "you might change your mind."

"Maybe," Ross said. "Anything can happen, but I wouldn't hold my breath if I was you."

Parmalee couldn't think of anything else worth saying, so he stepped down off the boardwalk and started across the street to the hotel.

Rex Cameron watched as Parmalee rode over to the hotel, dismounted and walked across to talk to Harry Ross. Ted Shea continued on, presumably to make arrangements at the undertaker's. It didn't occur to Cameron at that point that the stockyards were also that way.

Cameron thought that Parmalee was lying to him about Laura and Joey, but he couldn't be sure. If they were dead, he was going to have to make sure that Hankman and Walton got the blame for it.

He moved up in front of the saloon and

watched while Parmalee and Ross spoke. While he watched, he got an idea. One of his new men came to the door to speak to him, but he waved him away. When Parmalee walked away from Ross, Cameron called the man over.

"Krebs, remember what I said about convincing Hankman and Walton to leave town?"

"Yes, sir."

"Do you and the others have any qualms about makin' sure they *never* leave town?"

"Huh?"

Cameron spoke very clearly. "I want them dead."

Krebs said, "That'll cost more money."

"That's no problem."

"Then it's done."

"I'll be right back. Keep the men inside."

"Yes, sir. And Ross?"

"I've got other plans for Ross," Cameron said, and started across the street to put those plans into effect.

"He's comin' back," Hankman said.

"I can see him."

The two of them had been so fascinated by the meeting between the two gunmen that it had not occurred to them to move. Now they stood rooted to the spot as Parmalee crossed over to them. When he reached the boardwalk, he stepped up onto it, started for the hotel entrance, then stopped and turned his head toward them.

"It would be wise for the two of you to be gone by the time I come out."

With that, he turned and went inside.

Hankman and Walton exchanged a glance and then hurried across the street to talk to Ross.

"Are you gonna kill 'im?" Hankman asked.
"Yes."
"When?" Walton asked.
"As soon as he's rested."
"Rested?" Walton said. "Why don't you take him now, when he's tired?"

Ross pushed his hat up from his eyes so that he could look directly at Walton. "Why don't I just backshoot him and be done with it?" His tone was low, menacing.

"Well, what about Cameron?" Hankman asked.
Slowly, Ross moved his gaze from Walton to Hankman.
"I've thought about that."
"And?"
He smiled tightly and said, "And I don't like being manipulated."
"What's that mean?" Hankman demanded.
"It means that getting paid is your problem."
"What?" Walton said. ▪
Ross lowered his hat again and didn't speak.
"Ross—"
Ross simply raised his hand to cut Walton off, and then folded his hands over his stomach.
Hankman and Walton looked at each other helplessly, then turned and walked away.
"What are we supposed to do now?" Hankman said.
"Like the man said," Walton replied. "It's our problem. Let's figure out a way to solve it."

* * *

As Walton and Hankman crossed the street, Cameron walked toward Harry the Hat Ross, who seemed to be very much in demand today. Cameron had taken refuge in a doorway to give the other two time to plead their cases. Now it was his turn.

"Ross."

Ross tipped his hat up and said, "Foreman. What's on your mind?"

"You've got money comin'."

"So?"

"How'd you like to make a lot more?"

"How?"

"By killin' Parmalee."

Ross smiled and said, "I'm gonna do that anyway."

"Let's just call it a bonus, then."

Ross eyed the man and asked, "How much of a bonus?"

"Oh . . . let's say . . . five thousand dollars?" Cameron said. He was sure the old man would go for that much.

Ross, who had been prepared to shove Cameron's offer back into his face, paused. Since he was planning on killing Parmalee anyway, where was the harm in accepting this "bonus?" He had never seen five thousand dollars all in one place before.

"That's on top of what you already owe me, right?" He didn't want to appear too eager, so he made an effort to seem . . . businesslike.

"Of course."

Ross crawled back under his hat again and said, "You've got a deal."

"It has to be today, though," Cameron said, "or no deal."

After a moment, Ross said, "Right, today."

Cameron waited, but when Ross didn't speak again, he turned and walked back to the saloon. Now Hankman and Walton were taken care of, and so was Parmalee. That left only Ted Shea, and he would take care of Shea himself.

Parmalee got two hotel rooms and made sure that his overlooked the main street. He looked out the window now and saw Rex Cameron across the street, talking with Harry the Hat Ross.

Whatever sense of fair play Ross may have felt, Parmalee was sure that Cameron was offering him enough money to forget it.

So much for resting up.

CHAPTER THIRTY-NINE

It was when Cameron left Harry Ross that he suddenly realized that Ted Shea had not been going to any undertaker. He was heading to the stockyards to sell his beef. That meant that Laura and Joey were still alive. Cameron had to smile. Parmalee had played him just right, but it hadn't worked. Now that Cameron knew that Laura and Joey were still alive, he could concentrate on Ted Shea.

He started toward the other end of town, where the stockyards were.

"Thirty cents on the dollar," the man said. "That's the best I can do, Mr. Shea, I'm sorry."

Ted had spoken with four men so far, and thirty cents was the best offer he had gotten. The man making the offer was Carl Banks. The offer was fair, in that Ted had visions of having to sell the herd for ten cents on the dollar.

"Take the offer, my friend."

"I don't seem to have much of a choice." Ted extended his hand and shook hands with the man.

"Deal. I'll be out to your herd to inspect it in the morning."

"Do you have a couple of men I can hire to keep an eye on it? I've got my wife and daughter out there now, and I'd like to put them in the hotel."

"Sure," the man said. "I'll take care of it for you."

"Thank you."

"It's too bad you were late, Mr. Shea."

"Yeah," Ted said, "too bad for me, but good for you, eh?"

Banks spread his hands helplessly and said, "I'm a businessman, Mr. Shea."

"I understand that, Mr. Banks," Ted said. "I'll meet you at the herd in the morning."

Banks nodded. "I'll have two men out there within the hour."

"Thanks."

Ted left the man's office and found Rex Cameron waiting outside for him.

"Hello, Cameron."

"What'd you get?" Cameron asked. "Ten cents on the dollar? Twenty?"

"If I tell you," Ted said, "you'll head right for the telegraph office and send a telegram to my father-in-law. Forget it."

"I'll be sending him a telegram anyway," Cameron said, with a smile, "telling him he can expect his daughter and granddaughter home very soon."

Ted took a few steps forward until he was almost toe to toe with Cameron. "You even think about touching my family, Rex," he said, "and I'll kill you."

"Really?"

"Yes, really."

"What are you gonna do, send Parmalee after me?"

"Oh, no," Ted said. "Don't worry about that. I'll kill you myself. Keep that in mind."

"Well, that's good," Cameron said. "It's good that you're not going to rely on Parmalee, because he's not gonna be with us much longer."

"Step aside, Cameron."

"You think you're gonna get back home in one piece, Shea?"

"That's where I've got you, Rex," Ted said. "I'm not going home, and neither are Laura and Joey. You can tell your boss that. We won't be back. He's seen the last of his daughter."

"Mr. Venable's not gonna like that, Ted. I tell him that, he might just order me to kill you."

"Well, if he does," Ted said, "you take your best shot. All right?"

"Don't worry, Ted," Cameron said, "it won't take my best."

After Ted Shea left the stockyards, Cameron went to the telegraph office. He sent a telegram to his boss telling him that his daughter and granddaughter were fine, and that his son-in-law had no intentions of bringing them back. He waited for an answer.

When it came, it said exactly what he had expected it to say.

* * *

Ted went to the hotel to find Parmalee. Hankman and Walton were no longer hanging around out front. As he entered, Parmalee was coming down the steps.

"Here's the key to your room," Parmalee said, handing it to him. "I got you one with two beds."

"Thanks."

"Sell the cattle?"

"Yes," Ted said. "I got thirty cents on the dollar."

"That's better than we expected."

"It's nowhere near what we need to get on with our lives," Ted said.

"That remains to be seen. Did you get some men to watch the herd?"

"The buyer, Banks, is sending two men out."

"You might as well go out and bring back your wife and daughter."

"You're going to stay here?"

"That's right."

"Isn't that dangerous?"

"Did you see the man across the street?"

Ted walked to the door and looked across. "The one with the big white hat? Wait a minute, that's Ross?"

"That's him. Cameron was talking to him a little while ago."

"And?"

"And he's going to try to kill me sometime today," Parmalee said. "I don't want to be hard to find."

"So that's what he meant."

"Who?"

"Cameron. He came to see me at the stockyards. He told me not to rely on you too much, because you weren't going to be around much longer."

"Uh-huh. He must have offered Ross a lot of money."

"The old man's."

"We wouldn't want all that money to go to waste, would we?"

"What about the others?"

"I don't think we have to worry about the others," Parmalee said. "They seem to be having a disagreement with Cameron. They'll probably take care of each other."

"I don't think so," Ted said. "I think Rex and I have an appointment ourselves."

"He's got six guns behind him," Parmalee said. "I'll back you up after I take care of Ross."

Ted smiled. "That's an offer I won't turn down."

"Go and get your family, Ted," Parmalee said. "I'm sure they can use a good, long rest."

CHAPTER FORTY

Ted rode out to the herd and brought back Laura and Joey. While there, he met the two men Carl Banks had sent out, and satisfied himself that they were just a couple of cowhands, and not hired guns.

On the way back, he told Laura about selling the cattle, and the price he got.

"What will that come out to?" she asked.

"Not enough to save the ranch."

"To hell with the ranch, Ted."

He turned and looked at her. Joey was riding up ahead of them, out of earshot.

"It might be enough to save us, Laura," Ted said. "What do you think?"

Before she could answer, there was a shot, and Ted fell from his horse as if someone had yanked him.

"Ted!"

Joey turned and shouted, "Daddy!"

"Joey, get down!" Laura shouted.

Joey didn't listen. She turned her horse and rode back to her father. Only then did she dismount, as had her mother. Together they crouched over Ted, as if shielding him from further harm.

Parmalee was looking for a place to waste time. He decided not to sit in front of the hotel, because Ross was still seated across the street. He walked to the Lucky Nickel Saloon, but when he saw Hankman and Walton inside, he kept on going. He went instead to the Pretty Lady Saloon, entered and walked to the bar.

"What can I get for you?" the bartender asked.

"Beer," Parmalee said, "cold."

"Only kind we got," the man said. It turned out to be true, and Parmalee quickly finished his beer and ordered another.

Parmalee nursed the second beer from a table. He kept an eye on the people in the saloon, and noticed two or three men keeping an eye on him. It occurred to him that they were probably some of Cameron's hired men. They certainly didn't look like they made their living by the gun.

As it became later, the saloon got busier, and the girls began working the floor. Parmalee noticed that they were all very pretty, and figured the owner probably made a point of that, given the name of the place.

As time passed, some absences began to become very obvious. Ted Shea and his family weren't back yet, and Rex Cameron wasn't around. Parmalee finished his beer, got up and walked to the door. He turned his head before leaving and saw the same three men watching him. They hadn't made a move on him, probably because they hadn't been ordered to. He remembered being told that Cameron had hired half a dozen guns. Were they all here? Or were some of them with Cameron—wherever he was?

Parmalee left the saloon, and as he stepped down into the street, he saw three people riding in.

"Parmalee!" Joey shouted. "My dad's been shot!"

When the doctor came out, they all stood. Parmalee had his arm around Joey's shoulder. Laura's hands were clasped tightly together.

"How is he?" Parmalee asked.

"He'll be fine," the doctor said. "The bullet went through his side and doesn't seem to have hit anything vital. I've stopped the bleeding."

"Can he leave?"

"In a little while you can take him to the hotel," the doctor said. "He should rest now."

"Can I see him?" Laura asked.

"Sure."

"Me, too."

"No," Laura said, then she looked at Parmalee.

"Come on, Joey," Parmalee said, "why don't we get something to eat . . . in a restaurant. It's been a long time since we had a decent meal."

"Go on, honey," Laura said. "Daddy'll be fine."

Joey looked at the doctor, who nodded.

"Well, all right. I am a little hungry."

"Come inside, Mrs. Shea," the doctor said, and led the way.

Parmalee walked outside with Joey.

"Where are we gonna eat?" she asked.

"I don't know. It'll be dark soon. Let's just walk and find a place."

As they started to walk, she said, "Do you know who shot Pa?"

"No," Parmalee said, "not for sure."

"Do you think you know?"

"I think so."

"Will you kill him for me, whoever he is?"

Parmalee looked down at her and said, "You don't mean that, Joey."

"Yes, I do."

Before he could say anything else, someone shouted out, "Parmalee!"

He turned and saw Harry the Hat Ross standing across the street.

"Ross," Parmalee said, "not now."

"Now, Parmalee," Ross said. "I've said all along that it would be at my time, and my place."

"What's gonna happen?" Joey asked. "Is he gonna kill you?"

"He's going to try, honey," Parmalee said to her. To Ross he said, "Let the girl get to safety."

"I've got nothing against her," Ross replied.

"Run, Joey," Parmalee said. "All the way down the street."

"But, Parmalee," she said, "I don't want you to get shot, too."

"Go ahead," he insisted. "I'll be fine."

She still didn't want to go, and grudgingly gave ground. Finally she started running down the street, but she stopped and stepped into a doorway, from where she could still see what was going to happen.

Rex Cameron and three of his men returned to town just in time to see Parmalee and Ross facing each other.

"Good," Cameron said, dismounting, "I didn't miss it."

Up and down the street the word was getting out that Harry the Hat and Dan Parmalee were facing off.

A man burst into the doctor's office, looked around, then opened the door to his examining room, where the doctor was with Ted and Laura Shea.

"Hey, Doc, you gotta see this," the man called.

"Get out of here, you idiot!"

"Harry the Hat Ross and Dan Parmalee are gonna do it, in the street!"

"Get out!"

The man shrugged, turned and ran off to bring the news to someone more appreciative.

"Get me on my feet," Ted Shea said.

"What?"

"I have to get out there," Ted said, trying to swing his feet down from the table.

"What for?" the doctor said. "To get yourself shot again?"

"The doctor's right, Ted," Laura added. "You're staying here."

"Mrs. Shea is right—"

"Oh, my God," Laura cried suddenly, "what about Joey?"

"Parmalee wouldn't let anything happen to Joey," Ted said. "She's probably safe, but go out and see what's happening."

Laura rushed to the front door, ran outside and

down the street. She stopped when she saw the two men in the street.

"Changed your mind, eh, Harry?" Parmalee said. "What's the rush?"

"No rush, Parmalee," Ross said, "I'm just ready."

"Somebody must have offered you a lot of money for this," Parmalee said.

"Let's stop talking, Parmalee. I'm getting hungry."

They circled each other until they were both in the middle of the street. On both sides of the street people had come out to watch.

"You still have time to call this off, Ross," Parmalee said.

Ross shook his head. "There are too many people watching, and too much riding on this, Parmalee."

"This is stupid," Parmalee said, "but go ahead."

Joey tried to watch from the doorway, but there were too many people blocking her view, so she had to move out toward the street. Parmalee was standing with his back to her, Ross facing her.

Suddenly, Ross's hand streaked toward his gun. Parmalee drew his, but it seemed to her that he was moving very slowly, and then she heard two shots. . . .

CHAPTER FORTY-ONE

In the wake of the shooting, Rex Cameron chose to run into the Pretty Lady Saloon and surround himself with his men. It seemed the safest course of action.

Parmalee needed only a moment with the sheriff, who himself was one of the witnesses to the fact that the shooting was fair. When he turned, he was faced with both Laura and Joey.

"Are you all right?" Laura asked.

"You're bleeding!" Joey said.

Parmalee looked down at himself and saw some blood on his pants. Apparently Ross's bullet had creased his thigh.

"I'm fine."

"Come to the doctor's office," Laura said.

"No," Parmalee said, ejecting the spent shell from his gun and inserting a live one. "Now that the shooting has started, let's get it over with."

"What do you mean?"

"He's gonna kill the man who shot Pa."

"You know who shot Ted?" Laura asked.

"I believe it was Rex Cameron. I'm going to find him now."

"What if you're wrong, Parmalee?" Laura asked. "You could be killing an innocent man."

"Don't worry," Parmalee said. "I'll make sure I ask him before I kill him."

"Parmalee—"

"Take Joey and go back to the doctor's office," Parmalee said. "I'll come for you there, and we'll get something to eat."

"Right after you've killed . . . two men?"

Parmalee touched Laura's cheek and said, "It's hungry work."

Hankman and Walton had watched the proceedings from the sidelines, and were impressed.

"I never saw anyone draw that fast," Hankman said.

"Makes me glad I'm a backshooter," Walton confessed.

They both stared at the fallen Ross for a few moments. When he fell, Harry the Hat's white hat fell off, rolled on its wide brim for a few feet, and then settled down into the dirt.

"He'd shit if he could see his hat now," Hankman said.

* * *

Parmalee went directly to the Pretty Lady and entered. A group of men had to part in order for him to pass, and they then crowded into the saloon behind him, anxious to see whom he was going to shoot next.

To Parmalee's satisfaction, Rex Cameron was there.

"Cameron."

Cameron was sitting at a corner table, surrounded by his hired hands. "What do you want, Parmalee?"

"I missed you earlier when I was in here."

"I went for a ride," Cameron said. "Is that a crime?"

"That depends on what you did while you were riding," Parmalee said.

"What do you think I did?"

"I think you tried to kill Ted Shea."

"You can't prove that."

"Maybe I can't," Parmalee said, "but the sheriff can."

"How?"

"You've got six men here. I saw three of them earlier while you were riding. That means that the other three were with you. If the sheriff arrests all of you for attempted murder, don't you think one of them will give you up, rather than let the four of you go to prison?"

Parmalee saw a couple of the men exchange a glance, and knew he'd struck a nerve.

"You told Shea earlier today that he wasn't going to go back home," Parmalee said. "You tried to see to it that he didn't."

"He told *me* he wasn't going home."

"You tried to make sure of that," Parmalee said. "You also told him not to depend on me, that I wouldn't be around much longer. You used Ross to try to see to that. He didn't get the job done."

"Look—"

"Now I'm giving you another chance at it," Parmalee said. "A chance to do the job yourself."

"Myself?" Cameron said. "I'm not that foolish, Parmalee. I know I can't beat you, but can you beat all of us?"

Parmalee looked around the table at the men Cameron had paid. "I don't think I'll have to beat all of you, Cameron," he said. "Some of your men have already decided to fold their hands."

Cameron looked around the table quickly, but Parmalee didn't give him much time.

"Besides," he went on, "the first bullet will find you, anyway. Even if one of these gentlemen gets lucky, I'll take you and at least two of them with me."

Again, some of the men at the table looked around at each other. They were adept enough at administering strong-arm beatings, or ambushing someone, but this wasn't what they had bargained for.

"Let's do it, Cameron," Parmalee said. "Come on, I'll draw and let's see how many of your paid guns draw, as well."

"Now wait—"

"The time for waiting is over," Parmalee said. "You're wearing a gun; you'd better use it."

Parmalee drew his gun swiftly, and Cameron,

in a panic, leaned back in his chair and clawed at his. Parmalee fired very accurately, placing a bullet squarely in Rex Cameron's heart.

Not one other man at the table made a move for his gun.

"Get out of here, all of you," Parmalee said. "Your meal ticket is dead."

Together the six men rose and filed out past Parmalee, who half turned to watch them leave. When they were gone, he went and checked Cameron, assuring himself that the man was dead.

"Sorry, Rex," he said, "but this is the only kind of message Max Venable will understand."

CHAPTER FORTY-TWO

Two days later both Ted Shea and Parmalee were patched up—hobbling a bit, but patched up. Ted had consummated his deal with Carl Banks, and the cattle were no longer his responsibility—or problem.

When Felix Hankman and Preston Walton heard that Parmalee had killed Rex Cameron, they decided that they had spent enough time in Ellsworth—and in Kansas.

They took Parmalee's earlier advice, and left at first light the next morning.

Laura and Joey were sleeping late in their room, as they had done the day before. Ted and Parmalee were having breakfast together in the dining room of the hotel.

Ted passed an envelope across the table to Parmalee.

"What's this?"

"That's the fee we agreed on."

Parmalee drummed his fingers atop the envelope for a few moments, then passed it back.

"Hey—"

"I told you in the beginning why I was doing this," Parmalee said. "Keep the money."

"But you earned—"

"Just imagining the look on Venable's face when he got word of Cameron's death, and your telegram saying you wished him a good life, is fee enough for me."

"Parmalee—"

"Take the money, Ted, and use it for Joey. A gift from me to her, all right?"

Ted smiled and said, "Under those circumstances, I'll accept it."

"Good."

"You're not quite as cold as people think—or as you wish people would believe."

"I'm as cold as I have to be, Ted," Parmalee said. "Just ask Ross, or Cameron."

"Good point," Ted said. "I won't try to make you something you're not—or don't want to be."

"I'll tell you something I don't want to be anymore," Parmalee said, "and that's here." He stood up and asked, "What are you and your family going to do, Ted?"

"We're gonna try and *be* a family, Parmalee," Ted said. "We'll find someplace and settle down, and try to be satisfied with what we have."

"I wish you luck."

Ted stood up and shook hands with Parmalee.

"Aren't you gonna say good-bye to Joey?"

"She's asleep," Parmalee said, "and I want to get an early start. You say good-bye for me, okay?"

"If that's what you want, I will."

Parmalee nodded, then left the dining room, and the hotel.

Parmalee was in the livery, saddling his horse, when Joey came running in.

"You were gonna leave without sayin' goodbye," Joey accused.

"I didn't want to wake you," Parmalee said. "Did your father?"

"No," she said, "I woke on my own."

He pulled the cinch tight and turned to face her.

"Why do you have to go, Parmalee?" she asked. "Why can't you stay with us?"

"Joey," Parmalee said, "you don't even know where you're going to end up."

"You could let us know where you are," she said. "We could send you word where we end up living, and you could come and live with us."

"I can't do that, Joey," Parmalee said. "You, your father, your mother, you're a family. There's no room there for me."

"I'd make room for you."

He walked over to her, trailing his horse behind him.

"I know you would, Joey," he said, "and you don't know how much I appreciate that."

They faced each other for a few moments, and then she reached out and took a handful of his shirt front.

"Bend down here so that I can kiss you goodbye," she said.

Parmalee hesitated, then leaned over. Her arms went around his neck, and as she pressed her soft cheek to his, he closed his eyes. Just for a moment, with this little girl clinging to his neck, for the first time in years, he relaxed and allowed himself to feel—and then the moment passed.

Parmalee stood up. "Good-bye, Joey."

"Bye, Parmalee."

She stepped aside, and he walked his horse outside and mounted up. As he rode away, he heard her voice call out behind him, four words that would stay with him and keep him warm on cold nights.

"I love you, Parmalee."

THE LAST WAY STATION
KENT CONWELL

As soon as Jack Slade and his partner, Three Fingers Bent, arrive in the small Texas town of New Gideon, they know no one wants them there. There's been some rustling in the area, and folks aren't taking too kindly to strangers. But things don't get any better when Slade and Bent move on. The two don't get far before a posse from New Gideon rides up, accuses Bent of murder, and takes him back to face a judge. Slade knows he won't have much time before his partner hangs on a trumped-up charge, and there's only one way he can save his friend—he'll have to find the real killer himself!

ISBN 10: 0-8439-5928-2
ISBN 13: 978-0-8439-5928-4 $5.99 US/$7.99 CAN

RIDERS OF PARADISE

ROBERT J. HORTON

Clint and Dick French may be identical twins, but Clint's wild ways contrast sharply with his brother's more sophisticated tastes. But then Dick decides to share his brother's responsibilities at the family ranch—and ends up sharing his enemies as well. When notorious troublemaker Blunt Rodgers mistakes Dick for Clint, the tenderfoot looks to be doomed. Three shots are fired, Blunt ends up dead, and the sheriff doesn't need evidence to peg Clint the killer. And once word gets back to the infamous outlaw Blunt rode with, a whole gang of hardcases will be gunning for *both* brothers.

ISBN 10: 0-8439-5895-2
ISBN 13: 978-0-8439-5895-9 $5.99 US/$7.99 CAN

TROUBLE'S
MESSENGER

Peter Messenger is made for trouble. He is specially
trained in the art of death, even though he's never
killed anyone. But his skills with his hands, a gun, or
a knife are undeniable. And there is only one person
he plans to use them on: Summer Day, the wily med-
icine man who has tortured and killed a defenseless
white. But to get to the one he seeks, Peter will have
to take on the whole Blackfoot nation…and hope his
extraordinary talents are enough to stay alive against
the wrath of an entire tribe.

ISBN 10: 0-8439-5858-8
ISBN 13: 978-0-8439-5858-4 $5.99 US/$7.99 CAN